THE CHARING CROSS BOYS

Book One

Set **Fire** to the *Rain*

M. KATHERINE CLARK

Other Works
By M. Katherine Clark

The Greene and Shields Files
> Blood is Thicker Than Water
> Once Upon a Midnight Dreary
> Old Sins Cast Long Shadows
> Tales from the Heart, Novelettes

Love Among the Shamrocks Collection
> Under the Irish Sky
> Across the Irish Sea
> On the River Shannon
> The Land Across the Sea, an Emmet O'Quinn Short

Love Among the Shamrocks Collection the Next Generation
> In Dublin Fair City
> Song of Heart's Desire
> Chasing After Moonbeams

Love Among the Shamrocks Universe
> Take My Breath Away
> Ghosted – *Coming Soon*

The Charing Cross Boys
> Set Fire to the Rain
> Sweet Caroline
> I Put a Spell on You
> Hold Me Closer
> You Don't Own Me

The Wolf's Bane Saga
> Wolf's Bane
> Lonely Moon
> Midnight Sky
> Star Crossed
> Moon Rise
> Moon Song, a Companion Guide

Dragon Fire
> Heart of Fire
> Will of Fire
> Born of Fire – *Coming Soon*
> Land of Fire, a Novella – *Coming Soon*

Sherlock Holmes Family
> Soundless Silence, a Sherlock Holmes Novel
> The Rest is Silence, an Edmond Holmes Novel

MacCulloch Castle Ghosts
> Silent Whispers, a Scottish Ghost Story
> Silent Night, a Scottish Christmas Ghost Story

For all my fans, thank you for your support of my boys! I am so excited to share not only Collins and Sweets, but Rhys and Kiter's from Set Fire to the Rain; Boyd and Vidar in I Put a Spell on You; Gareth, Dae-Hyun, and Lamont in Hold Me Closer; and finishing The Charing Cross Boys series Callum and Killian in You Don't Own Me! I love being able to write something you all enjoy!

Trigger Warnings:

There is some language from several homophobic characters that the author condemns in the strongest terms but it is written for the understanding of the characters and hatred the LGBTQ+ community experience daily.

There are also conversations around previous cheating and though there is no cheating on the page, the character has cheated in the past and the conversation that surrounds them talking it out does occur. There is also the loss of a loved one on page. Gun violence and abuse.

If any of these are triggers for you, please proceed with caution.

Prologue

Colonel Sommerset Kiter looked up at the door of the café as it jingled open. The man he was there to meet shook the raincoat that was drenched from the late summer downpour still clouding the outside. Baseball cap, black Henley, tight blue jeans, and black biker boots, and Sommerset swallowed the drool that threatened to escape.

Rhys Campbell or *Leo* as his codename was known for the past fifteen years, was always a handsome man, but in that outfit, he looked edible. His pale blue eyes looked up and scanned the area. Lighting on Kiter, he motioned with his chin in greeting and stalked across the room. Kiter's eyes tracked the movement and stayed frozen on his back as he stood in line to order. Even though he couldn't hear over the din of conversation and the pounding of rain on the roof and windows, Sommerset knew his order like the back of his hand. It hadn't changed in twenty-five years.

"Large Cinnamon Dolce Latte, nonfat whip, skim milk, and an extra shot of espresso. Oh... and a coffee cake."

The smell of cinnamon was always nostalgic for him and as the chair across from him filled with all six foot three inches of hulking Scottish muscle, Kiter took a deep breath filling his senses with cinnamon. Leo leaned back in the chair, legs spread, boots flat on the ground, right arm on the arm of the chair, hand resting on his thigh, pointer finger of his left hand tracing the handle of the coffee mug, eyes fixed on Kiter.

"So..." he began, then paused, his righthand palm flashing up in a shrug. "What's this about?"

And that voice brought a thousand memories with it.

Clearing his throat, Kiter leaned forward over his white porcelain coffee cup. It was nearly empty as he had drunk the first one too quickly, but the smell of just black coffee was... off when mixed with the other smells around him. Still, he dropped his eyes to stare at the inky black of the bitter drink and took a breath gathering his thoughts.

"I-ehm-wanted to thank you."

Leo said nothing, prompting him to continue. "Thank you for everything you did for Geoff and the girl."

"Corinne."

"Right, sorry, I didn't remember her name. My focus was on Geoff."

"Always is," Leo scoffed and took a sip of his coffee.

"Can we not?" Kiter sighed.

"Not what?" Leo's voice was dripping with sarcasm.

"Not do this? Yes, okay? I know you never liked Geoff. I never did understand why."

"No? Well, let me clarify."

"Let's not, not here."

"Oh, no," Leo shook his head. "You wanted to know. So I'll tell you."

"Leo…"

"Did you forget? Because you clearly forgot about me, about us, when you let him suck you off. And later when you pounded his arse into *our* bed? Did you forget that too?" Leo demanded.

"How many times? We were on a break. You had been deployed. What was I supposed to do? Wait for you?"

"Usually when one is in a relationship that's what you do," Leo answered.

"We weren't in a relationship at that time, remember? Christ, Leo. And it wasn't Geoff's fault, okay? He didn't know we were together. He hated me when he found out."

"Oh, you poor thing." His sarcasm was always something Kiter loved, but he hated it then.

"Look, I don't want to talk about this," Kiter said.

"Oh, I'm sorry my dislike of the man you cheated on me with isn't something you like discussing."

Kiter heaved a sigh. "This was a mistake."

Leo grabbed his coffee and coffee cake. "Couldn't have said it better myself." He stood.

"Wait, please," Kiter tried. "Leo, please, just wait. Can we talk?"

"About what? Hmm? You already thanked me for helping out. It's my job, so what?"

"I was hoping we could…"

Leo stared at him for a long moment. "Could? What?"

3

"Just talk like we used to."

"That's the problem, Scorpio, we're not who we used to be. And we'll never be able to be who we used to be again. Now, you're welcome. Consider it over, okay?" Leo said.

"Rhys..."

"Don't," Leo's eyes went fiery, and his body hardened. "You lost that right a long time ago. Go back to him, if he'll have you. There's nothing for you here."

Kiter closed his eyes after he saw Leo stalk toward the counter asking for his coffee and cake to be transferred to a disposable cup and bag. After a second, the chimes overhead jingled and Kiter knew he was gone. His commanding presence was no longer in the room. Letting out a sigh, he rested his forehead against his fingers and used his thumb to massage his temple where a headache grew. With a huff, he pulled off his glasses and rubbed his eyes.

Rhys Campbell, code name Leo for his Zodiac, had been his best friend since they were boys. When Kiter's father had been stationed at Kinloss in the remote northeast of Scotland, Kiter had been twelve and hated every second of it. Until he met scrawny, awkward, and adorable Rhys from next door. They were within a year of each other and both their fathers worked at the airbase though in different capacities. They spent the summers and holiday breaks from school trapezing around the Highlands finding and discovering new-to-them places, caves, and glens. They swam in the freezing waters of the North Sea, then raced all the way to old Mrs. Tibbins' Café to get a hot piece of soda bread and stew. As they grew up, Kiter realized his feelings for his best friend were more than platonic. And one day, near his fifteenth birthday, he kissed him. Rhys had frozen and Kiter was certain he had just lost his best friend, but then something happened... Rhys kissed him back.

Sitting in the café in London watching the boy turned man, walk out of his life, Sommerset Kiter longed for the past. The past where they would sneak around, stay out too late, crawl in and out of their windows just to steal a kiss, a hug, a cuddle. To be able to go back to the time where the worst thing imaginable was explaining love bites on their necks to their older brothers or getting caught in the act by their parents. Not the separation that grew between them, not the hurt and anger in Leo's eyes, not the pain he caused.

He missed him, his best friend, his second-in-command. Forgiveness was not available, and Kiter knew Leo would never forget. So, how to make amends? He had no idea. But he would do anything in his power to make it up to him. Starting with a phone call. Taking out his mobile, he pulled up the number he needed.

"O'Grady," the man answered.

"Scorpio here, I've got your first recruit, Special Agent, if you're interested," Kiter said.

"I'm listening, boss."

Chapter One

The pub was loud when Leo opened the door and it nearly deterred him when he remembered it was Trivia Night. All he wanted was a beer or ten and to lick his proverbial wounds in peace. Sommerset Kiter knew how to get under his skin. He was a master at making Leo remember things he thought he had killed and buried decades ago. But no. One solo meeting and Leo was back to the twenty-five-year-old who came home from deployment to find his best friend/boyfriend/lover in bed with some barely legal cadet. His words still hurt, even after all those years.

"What does it matter? We were on a break, Rhys. How was I supposed to know you wanted me to wait for you? You were probably sleeping with anyone over there. God knows you're not picky."

But he was. He was very picky. At that time, Sommerset Kiter was his first and only. The stupidly in love part of him thought they would be together forever. But Kiter proved him wrong. It was another ten years until he saw him again and even then, Leo wanted the nightmare to end. He had been recruited at thirty-three, the height of his military career, into the Special Reconnaissance Regiment of Her Majesty's Military. It was his dream. But sorting into the best covert team called The Zodiacs, he didn't imagine Kiter would be selected too... and as their commander. He and Kiter had locked eyes across the room and Rhys' stomach clenched in agony. The man he loved more than life, his best friend and his greatest pain was his commander. The man he had to trust with his life. The man he would take orders from was the man he couldn't forget, staring at him in horror when he walked into their bedroom after eleven months in Afghanistan.

He needed a drink after all the memories surfaced after coffee that morning. And as Rhys slid onto the barstool waiting for the man behind the bar to walk over, he admitted to himself, he was tired. Tired of... everything. He hated his past with Kiter because it was everywhere. He loved his military career but that had been shot to hell five years ago when the line holding him to the Helo broke and he fell thirty feet breaking his back and leg in two places. Surgery and physical therapy for months afterward and a medical discharge from the military and he was finally away from Kiter, but at what cost?

"Hey gorgeous, what can I get ya?" the sound of a male voice in front of him drew him out of his little pity party.

"Whisky, neat, and a lager."

"Comin' up, handsome." The man did a fancy flip with a beer glass and began pouring. "Chasin' away demons?"

Leo nodded. "Something like that."

"Well, you're in luck. We've got just the thing. Trivia night is best for a distraction."

"No thanks. Just want some quiet. I'll take my drinks to the other room."

The man shook his head. "Sorry, gorgeous, we got the band set up in the other room. No quiet place tonight."

Leo sighed a heavy breath as the man placed a whisky and beer in front of him. Tossing back the whisky, Leo reveled in the burn, but he was far from where he wanted to be. Taking the beer, he took a few hefty sips then ordered another whisky. The bartender, a young man, probably early twenties if he was a day over nineteen, was clean shaven, with cuttable cheek bones and jaw, curly brown hair cut short on the sides and Leo saw the faintest glimpse of a braid tattoo on his wrist. Those grey eyes were sinful and the look he was giving Leo with those pouty full lips and freckles across his nose should have been illegal.

"I know a place that's quiet," he said suggestively.

"Let me guess, your place?" Leo offered.

"Nah, I got roommates, but yours... I'm sure would be very quiet."

Leo couldn't help himself, he breathed a laugh. "What's your name, kid?"

"Kid?" the man questioned. "I'm far from a kid. But the name's Boyd."

"Boyd," Leo repeated. "What makes you think I'd be interested? Or even swing that way?"

"One, have you seen me?" Boyd asked. "Everyone's interested. Two, have you seen you? You're gorgeous and looking at me like you're starving and I'm a piece of filet. Which, let's face it, I kinda am."

Leo tossed back the second whisky without breaking

eye contact with him. "I'm a vegetarian."

"Liar. You don't get a physique like that by eating tofu."

Leo stared. The kid was different than what he usually liked or even took home for a one-night stand. And after all the years he had nameless hookups, he never looked forward to... the *conversation*. He usually didn't tell anyone because it was different than what people expected. He knew what everyone assumed. He was a top. Or at least versatile. And he was... somewhat. At least, he had grown to be, but his heart was always bottoming and it had been nearly two years since he had someone interested in him that way. One look at the kid, half his size, half a foot shorter and there was no way Boyd was a top. But then he felt guilty about assuming and was tired of lying about himself.

"Thanks, kid. I'm good."

The look on his face was priceless. It was clear the kid wasn't used to rejection. But soon, he shrugged and turned away.

"Your loss."

Indeed it was. Though he may prefer to bottom, Leo wasn't dead and as Boyd turned, flashing that sweet ass hugged in black skinny jeans, Leo kicked himself. It hadn't been too long since his last hookup and he wasn't fooling himself, he and Boyd would have one hell of a night, but he wasn't sure he could go through another disappointing one night stand just to feel good for about an hour or so.

Mic feedback rang in his ears as the trivia moderator stepped up to the podium. The headache that always started behind his eyes ever since his fall began and he knew he was done for the night. Finishing his beer, he took out his wallet and set a £50 note on the counter under the empty glass. He looked up to see a different man behind the bar. The cute Boyd was no where to be found. Disappointment and annoyance set in as Leo slid off the seat and made his way out the door not nearly buzzed enough to forget about his earlier conversation with Kiter.

As soon as he pushed opened the door, the fresh air mixed with cigarette smoke hit his nose. He paused and took in the dark sky and heaviness of the air around him. The rain had stopped for a couple hours but from the ache in his leg, he knew it would start up again soon.

"Early night considering you came here to forget." The voice was near him but came from the shadows.

"Busy last couple days," he admitted.

"Work? Lovers?"

"Yes to both."

Boyd stepped out of the darkness and into the halo of light pouring out of the windows of the pub. He flicked his cigarette into a puddle of rainwater. Leo held in his chuckle. He could fine the guy £2500 if he wanted to. But he wouldn't. He mentally shook his head, maybe that made him a bad cop. *Who cares?* He berated himself.

"Which one you trying to forget? Work or lover?" Boyd asked.

"Yes."

"Both?" Boyd shook his head and tsked. "I heard of guys married to the job but you're taking it to the next level when you're sleeping with the job."

"Smart arse," Leo grumbled.

"You in a relationship?"

Leo watched him, but eventually answered. "No."

"What sort of work do you do?"

Again, Leo watched him. "Retrievals." He smirked. He was rather proud of that answer. It wasn't wrong. He was Police Special Ops and most of his cases were retrievals. Just the object they retrieved varied. "My turn. How old are you?"

"How old do you want me to be?" Boyd answered.

"Well... if we're gonna do this then, legal."

"I'm legal."

"Got proof of that?" Leo asked.

Boyd scoffed and pulled out his wallet. Handing over the ID, Leo breathed a sigh of relief when he saw Boyd was twenty-one but still... twenty-one, he was literally half Leo's age.

"Problem?" Boyd asked.

Leo debated all of two seconds before handing the ID back, not checking the last name. *No need,* he thought. The less they knew about each other the better. "No. My place is walking distance."

A salacious grin spread across Boyd's lips. "Lead the way."

Chapter Two

Leo woke to the sound of rain pelting his window frame and a throbbing in his leg. The injured bone hurt when it rained, it was like he had his own personal meteorologist. Groaning as his back spasmed too, he rolled from his side to his back and stared up at the ceiling. Memories of the previous night entered his mind and despite himself, Leo smirked. Boyd was fun. Skilled in many different areas and for the first time in a long time, he felt... sated.

He was alone in the flat, he knew that, but he didn't remember Boyd leaving. Somewhat disappointed he couldn't thank him with breakfast, Leo grunted and swung his legs over the side of the bed. Taking a second to wake up, he scratched his chest and stretched his back. Gazing out to the Thames, he enjoyed waking up to the water's gentle roll.

Standing slowly, he reached for his glasses and watch.

When his hand met only his glasses on the nightstand, his brow furrowed. He grabbed them and slid them on. His watch was gone. *Odd,* he thought. But it wasn't uncommon for him to take it off in the living room and since it was where their activities the previous night had started, it was highly possible he had tossed it onto the counter. Shrugging, he went to the en-suite. As he washed his hands, he opened the medicine cabinet to get his Vicodin. But the medication bottle wasn't there. He knew for a fact he had placed it back in there the night before after their second round. A sick feeling began to pulse in his stomach as he hurried into the living room and sure enough, his wallet and keys were missing. He glanced at the wall and breathed a sigh of relief; his Katana was still mounted over the fireplace with his father's military medals encased below but the painting covering his wall safe had been moved and the safe's door stood wide open and empty.

"Son of a bitch," he cured and searched for his phone. The old flip phone was still on the kitchen island along with his shirt from the night before. Apparently Boyd was skilled in *other* areas too.

"Idiot," Leo muttered shaking his hand as he dialed the police. He was never going to live it down when the lads from his department found out.

Three hours and several rounds of ribbing from his peers later, Leo stepped out onto London's streets. The robbery division had no hope in retrieving his stuff. Boyd had several last names and was apparently infamous in certain circles. Even when Leo gave them the name of the pub where he supposedly worked, there was little hope. Boyd had a known MO. Work at a pub for a few weeks, find a mark, flirt, get taken home, sex, steal, disappear, repeat. And Leo was just one in a long line of blokes to fall for the con.

They put out an APB on the missing items but had no hope in recovering the stolen money from his wallet and safe. Fortunately it wasn't more than a couple thousand, but he wanted his watch back. It was a gift from his SRR team on his retirement. He felt naked without it.

He walked down the road going nowhere in particular. His car had been taken, likely stripped for parts by then and all his credit cards. Fortunately, he was able to cancel them and report the few hundred pounds withdrawn from a bank machine as fraudulent. But with no car, no money, no access to his funds as the banks figured out what to do with his frozen accounts, and nowhere to go, he paused along the banks of the Thames. Gazing into the brown water, he was almost tempted to end it all but then the thought of inhaling the disgusting grime and trash was not appealing. Neither was going home. It felt… violated. He felt… violated. His trust. His sanctuary had been ripped apart.

The swirling waters of the Thames rippled as if laughing at him.

"Tough break." He jumped when he heard a voice beside him. Glancing over to see a man with dark brown hair standing to his right, Leo rolled his eyes and looked away but the man didn't get subtle, it seemed.

"What do you want, mate? I've already been robbed. I don't have anything left."

"Well, that's not true, is it?" the man said.

"Do I know you?"

"No," the man answered. "But I know you, Rhys Campbell. My name is O'Grady. Callum O'Grady and I'm putting together a team."

"A team? What sort of team?"

Callum turned to him. "Covert ops, Top Secret Missions, spy shit."

After a beat, Leo scoffed. "Okay, sure, mate. Look, Bedlam is off A232. Get some help for your delusions." Leo turned and stalked away.

"Leo," he called him back and Rhys froze hearing his callsign. Turning back, he saw Callum walk up to him slowly. "Have lunch with me. Best case scenario, I'm telling the truth and you can get back into what I know you love. With your martial arts and tongue for languages, you are wasted as a Police Special Operations. Worst case scenario, I am crazy, and you have to had lunch with a crazy person. The question is, is two hours of your life worth finding out?"

"You... want to recruit me?"

"Any reason I shouldn't?" Callum asked.

"Ehum... I'm forty-three and crippled."

"You're not crippled and though there may be some physical training needed, it's nothing you can't do. You're strong, fit, and have an excellent ear for languages. We need a man of your... abilities on our team. Your martial arts alone would interest even the Yanks. Yes, so you made an error in judgement last evening, who hasn't?"

Leo started. "You know what happened to me?"

Callum nodded. "I made Boyd at the pub last night."

Leo stared. "How long have you been following me?" He

questioned softly.

"Twenty-four hours. I wasn't going to take a friend's word about you. I needed to see you for myself."

"A friend?"

"Do you remember the woman you helped save from the Rossi family?"

"Corinne," he answered.

"That's right. Do you remember her boyfriend's name?"

"Lachlan O'Quinn."

Callum smirked. "Nothing wrong with your memory. I am Lachlan's younger brother's best friend. But that is my other life outside of MI6 so I would appreciate you not mentioning that to anyone. But the O'Quinns, especially Oisín, my friend, wouldn't shut up about you."

Leo remembered the six-foot-five-inch Irishman who hulled in the corner watching everything. "Okay, say for a moment, I do believe you. You have names, dates, and know things about me, however it wouldn't be hard to find out I'm good with languages as I'm a member of a lot of clubs. But say I do believe you; you expect me to believe you want me on your team after last night's shot show? I was taken in by a known grifter and lost nearly everything today."

Callum shrugged. "We all make mistakes. And I do believe you weren't in your right mind after your meeting with Colonel Kiter."

Leo stared. "You know about me and Kiter?"

"Yes."

Rhys was quiet.

"Ask what you really want to ask," Callum offered.

"I haven't been in the closet for nearly three decades. Is

this team of yours accepting?"

"Yes," Callum answered. "So, how about it?"

Rhys debated. On the one hand, he hadn't been happy at his job for a while and could do with a change. He was bored. There was no challenge anymore. He led a great team, but was it enough for him? He already knew the answer was no before he finished his thought. His work in the military and in SRR specifically was exciting, invigorating. What he was doing then meant something. His work as ground leader for the police special ops, wasn't bad, but it wasn't where his heart truly belonged. He wasn't sure when he started trusting Callum, but it was somewhere between him calling him his code name and telling him about his relationship with the O'Quinns.

"How many are on his team of yours?" Leo asked.

"With you? Two. You and me."

"You're joking right?"

"No, you'll be my first recruit."

"Not really selling the whole experience, O'Grady."

Callum shrugged. "We all got to start somewhere, Rhys."

"Leo," he corrected. "I haven't been Rhys in nearly twenty years."

"Okay, Leo then, so about that lunch?"

Against his better judgement, Leo found himself nodding. "Okay... woo me."

Callum grinned. "I'll leave that to Boyd," he winked.

With a self-deprecating chuckle, Leo walked with Callum to a small café and listened to his proposition.

Chapter Three

Callum: Leo is a go.

Kiter stared at the text message he had received an hour ago while he sat in on a department budgeting meeting. Leo had joined the team. Why wasn't he happy about that? Staring at the file on Boyd, the con artist who should have never looked twice at his man, Kiter wanted to throw something against the wall.

All they had was grainy surveillance footage of the famous thief, but it was enough of a picture to see Leo and several other marks be taken in and leave the various pubs with the kid. Kiter knew what happened after that and it settled in his stomach like bad tripe. The Leo… no the *Rhys* he knew would never be taken in by a pretty face, let alone take a stranger back to his place and… Kiter shook his head. He didn't want or need the mental images of Leo and Boyd having sex. How would that even work? They were both bottoms... Unless Leo switched over the years. Or could Boyd be a top? Kiter again, shook his head, that thought didn't help his unwanted mental images.

He would find Boyd and get Leo's things. At least everything Boyd hadn't already sold or used. The grifter conned the wrong man.

Leaning forward, he pressed the call button on his phone to his administrative assistant's desk.

"Yes, Colonel?" She answered.

"Could you get me tech on the phone, please Marjorie?" He asked.

"Right away, sir."

The phone went quiet, and Kiter waited impatiently. He certainly did *not* stare at the grainy image of Leo walking with Boyd and think of everything the two of them did that evening. He didn't consider himself a possessive man, nor did he think truly he had done anything wrong by sleeping with someone else. They were on a break. He shook his head. Who was he kidding? He and Rhys had been together since they were fourteen. They had argued the day before Rhys was set to deploy. Kiter didn't remember why they fought only that Rhys had said... or had it been him?... they needed a break. When the seventeen-year-old cadet Geoffrey Ainsley had thrown himself at Kiter, who was he to refuse? He and Rhys weren't together. So, why did he feel shitty about it at that moment?

"I have Tech on the line for you, Colonel." His admin's voice brought him back to the present.

"Thank you." The sound of her clicking off the phone and of someone breathing was the only indication he had been connected to Tech.

"Colonel Kiter?" A new voice spoke.

"Yes."

"This is Agent Yellen, sir. What can I do for you?"

"I need you to run a face for me. It's grainy but I need to get a clean picture and figure out where this guy is in London."

"Shouldn't be too difficult. Do you have the surveillance picture or CCTV footage?"

"I do."

"Let me remote into your computer and we can get it in real time."

Kiter approved Tech's request to remote in his computer and leaning back, watched as the agent took over his screen. Soon, the grainy pictures of Boyd with the men he conned came into focus. The only issue was he always seemed to know where the camera was and all they ever got was a partial face.

"Is it enough to get a full face?"

"Which man, sir?"

"The smaller one."

The agent made a noncommittal noise. "Let me try. But I doubt it. He's always wearing that beanie and the scarf is pulled up. It's like this guy knows where the cameras are."

"Well, he's a grifter, so…"

"Ah, makes sense. Let me try to work some magic."

That was the problem, no one but the men Boyd had slept with knew what he looked like. Kiter told the agent to do what he could then pulled out his phone.

Kiter: Did Rhys sit with a sketcher?

The text took a second to come through but when it did he spoke to the agent. "One of the victims sat with a police sketch artist. Would that help?"

"It would definitely help fill in parts of the face. I can tweak the sketch to look more human with some software I have. My sister works at the British Museum in the archeological department. She uses this to recreate faces from their skulls and paintings or sculptures. It's pretty neat."

"I'll get you the sketch then." Kiter was on the phone with the agent for the better part of two hours but by the time he was done, they had a few positive outcomes. There were about three hundred men answering to the vague description of Boyd in the greater London area. There were more but they were able to estimate his height and weight in comparison to Leo's and were able to filter out IDs that were over six feet tall and over or under the weight they estimated. They were still generous in Kiter's opinion. There was no way the guy was more than one-fifty, and he couldn't be a millimeter over five-eight. But the tech said the picture wasn't clear enough to be able to be exact and Boyd went by many names so even that wouldn't help.

After the tech saved all the pictures of possible matches on his computer, Kiter thanked him and hung up. He opened the file and stared at the photos. Clicking on some, he looked through them all and eliminated the ones he knew weren't right. He knew Rhys. Even if it had been nearly two decades since they were together, he knew what he liked and what he didn't like. What caught his eye and what didn't. His top few things were personal hygiene, clean cut - he blamed his military background for that even though Leo had a closely cropped beard, and not perfect. Rhys liked little imperfections in a lover. Kiter fought a smile remembering when he had gotten a scar on his eyebrow causing the hair to not grow there and Rhys would kiss it all the time saying how sexy it made him look. He liked those little things.

Kiter created two folders on the computer; one marked *Maybe* the other marked *Probably.* Each face he placed in the *Probably* folder tightened his stomach. He hated them all for no other reason than they had the potential of sleeping with the man Kiter still loved.

He froze on one picture, not even seeing it, as a realization came to him. If he hated the *potential* lovers, how did Rhys feel seeing the actual man Kiter cheated on him with? Geoffrey Ainsley was still in his life and even though there was nothing remotely sexual between them then, the point was it had happened. And Rhys had seen it. And to know Kiter and Ainsley were still friends, were still seeing each other as friends, knowing Kiter still thought of him, helped him when needed, hell, maybe even still cared for him, was something Rhys couldn't stomach.

"My god," he breathed. It finally all made sense. "Rhys... I'm... I'm so sorry." He grabbed his phone to call him and apologize, but he knew it would do no good. He needed to find Boyd, get Rhys his things back, and then attempt to apologize. Ainsley was still a friend even though he was in a committed relationship with his partner Peter Carlisle. Kiter wasn't willing to give up his friendship simply because Leo didn't like it, but he was willing to talk it out with both men. Carlisle's reaction to finding out Kiter and Geoff had been together still stuck in his mind. Carlisle didn't like him as much as Rhys didn't like Geoff. "So no euchre nights together, obviously." He chuckled setting his phone down. Although, he was fairly certain Rhys and Peter

Carlisle would get along famously.

He looked up when his phone rang on his desk. "Yes, Marjorie?"

"Commander Lester to see you, sir. He doesn't have an appointment, but he promises it'll only be a few minutes of your time."

"Send him in," he said and clicked out of his files, locking his computer, Standing as the head of his department entered, he greeted him. "Commander, sir, what a pleasant surprise." He indicated the chair opposite him. "To what do I owe the pleasure?"

"I wanted to check in, Kiter, see how things were progressing with the team," Lester shook his hand and sat opposite. The man was older than Kiter. His actual age was not known but Kiter put him around sixty-five. His wispy gray hair was thinning but didn't look badly on him. He had recruited Kiter out of the military two years ago and always came around to check in unannounced.

"Things are going well. We have one new recruit and I have my eye on two more."

"Anyone in particular?" Lester asked.

"Actually yes, sir. I don't know if you'll know them, but they're a Royal Marine and a Paratrooper. Captain Hesler and Commander Darius."

"Aren't they a couple?"

"I believe so, sir," Kiter answered. "It appears they have been partners for about seven years."

"Yes, I know of Commander Darius. Good choice, Colonel. Have you spoken to them yet?"

"They're currently out on assignment, sir, but I have

O'Grady ready to approach them when they return."

"And O'Grady? How is he doing?"

"He's a wonderful team leader, sir. Empathetic and firm. I enjoy working with him." Kiter leaned back.

"Good, I'm glad to hear it." Lester paused for a moment and Kiter observed him.

"Forgive me, sir, but I can't help feeling there's more to this visit than a simple check in that could have been done over the phone."

Lester chuckled. "I curse those observational skills of yours, Kiter."

"It's a gift, sir."

"It's damn annoying, is what it is,"

"Yes, sir, sorry, sir," Kiter grinned. "But please, tell me what is worrying you."

With a huffed sigh, Lester continued. "There's an op I need the Charing Cross Boys on. And it's time sensitive. Three months."

Kiter prevented his reaction of surprise and merely nodded slowly encouraging him to continue.

"I know it's short noticed especially with the lack of a team, But I would not mention it if it were not of the utmost importance."

"Of course, sir. What are the specs?"

"A British citizen, expat, is accused of selling British nuclear information to the Middle East and Russia. He is living in the Maldives and since extradition takes too long, MI6 wants to pull him out ourselves. Get him into Australian Waters and call the Coast Guard to pick him up."

"And our extraction?"

"You will take a boat to the agreed upon location where a British sub will pick you up in international waters and transport you home."

"Seems simple enough," Kiter said. "Why us? Why not another more established team?"

"Because it is simple enough and it would give your team a good chance to prove themselves. I can tell you, a few of the stuffies upstairs are looking for any reason to shut down your team."

"Why?" Kiter's brows furrowed.

"A group of gay or bisexual men proving they are better at everything than our own military? I'll leave it up to your imagination as to why. We may be living in the 21st century, Sommerset but several of those men are stuck in the 15th. This is just the case needed to prove them wrong. And to prove that you are as good of a leader as I know you are."

"Are they questioning my abilities?"

"It's... been thrown out. They're bigots, don't let them get to you."

Kiter nodded slowly again, his mind whirling with the possibilities, The foundation of the Charing Cross Boys was to be the British Government's answer to Diversity and Inclusion. Not that it would do much since on paper they didn't exist. But it made the ancient ones in Parliament and the virtue signalers feel better about themselves. But Kiter knew there would be some holdouts. Geoff's father, the Duke of Torrington being one of the more vociferous members.

"Well, then, I'll get on the phone with O'Grady and have him ramp up our recruitment. The paperwork is what's killing us. The transfer papers are getting put on hold for active military members."

Lester shrugged. "Who said they all had to be military? You have a diverse need, if a policeman, intelligence operative, hell, even a civilian meets your needs, don't hesitate."

With that, Lester stood, offered his hand to Kiter who promptly stood and shook it. "I know you won't let me down, Sommerset. You're perfect for this role. Speaking of, how's that hottie you were dating a few months back?"

Kiter had to remember who he was talking about. He hadn't had a boyfriend in years but there was one he dated for more than two months, and Lester had met him at a restaurant by accident. "Oh, ehm, do you mean Demetrius?"

"Yes, always thought it was a funny name. Reminded me of Shakespeare."

"We were just friends, sir."

"Who slept together?"

"Something like that," Kiter answered. He liked to keep his personal affairs... personal.

"Damn shame. He was handsome. What was he? Greek? Lebanese?"

"Syrian," Kiter answered.

"Invite him to our party, unless you're dating someone else now?"

"Party?" Kiter questioned.

"Yes, we're having a gathering to christen the CCB Team next week. Didn't you get the invite?"

"I must have yes," Kiter covered. He told Marjorie to always toss out invitations like that. He had no intention of ever attending anything. He hated crowds for one, and he hated the fakery that came with governmental parties.

"Good, well, invite him to come along."

"I don't think that would be appropriate, sir. He's dating someone else."

"Ah, I see, well get yourself a plus one even if you have to hire one." He chuckled. "Let's make those stuffies upstairs squirm."

"Squirm, sir?"

"Must I spell it out for you, Colonel? Get yourself a Rent Boy for the evening if you must and slap the oldies with some Gay PDA. I want them all to have their faces rubbed in it when you and the team return victorious."

"I see. Well, I'll see what I can do, sir."

"Good, excellent. Well, if you need me, you know where I work. And if I don't see you before the party, good luck in your search."

"Thank you, sir."

Kiter walked Lester to the door and waved goodbye as he left the department. Glancing at Marjorie who was looking at him expectantly, he shrugged. She feigned a smirk and opened the top drawer of her desk, pulling out a large gold envelope.

"Your invitation, sir." She grinned.

He rolled his eyes but sighed. "My schedule?"

"Clear, I made sure."

"Fine, RSVP for me." He turned to go back into his office and heard her call him back.

"It includes a plus one. Should I go through your little black book to find someone appropriate or do you want to take Commander Lester up on finding a Rent Boy for the evening."

"Very funny, Marjorie." He snapped back playfully.

"I can dress up for the evening, boss if you're desperate!"

She called as the door closed. He caught it and pulled it open popping his head out.

"When have you ever known me to be desperate?"

She grinned. "So no plus one, got it."

"Smartarse," he muttered as he shut the door hearing her chuckle.

Lester meant well... he thought. But sometimes Allies got a little too... Ally-ie. Kiter was out and proud about his sexuality. Generations of men before him were never able to be who they truly were and Kiter felt a strong sense of kinship with them. So once he was out at fifteen he never looked back. He couldn't have asked for better parents or siblings. His parents ended relationships with aunts and uncles who spoke out against him and to that day his mum, dad, and brother tried to set him up on dates and went to Pride Parades. But as much as he was grateful and no matter how much they loved Rhys, he would never be the flamboyant type it looked like Lester wanted and needed for the party. He never enjoyed making anyone uncomfortable especially with his sexuality. He always enjoyed subtleties of a plus one. Catching his eye across the room, smiling, promising all manner of unholy things as soon as they were alone. But to share PDA with a stranger, it would be an act and Kiter was good at acting. But who would he get?

Walking over to his desk, he sat down and logged back in to his computer nearly forgetting what he had been working on before Lester came in. But as soon as the faces of the men he was profiling came on screen, his stomach clenched. Rhys. Rhys had been duped and hurt, maybe not physically, but in all other ways. His sanctuary had been ripped from him. Violated in the most intimate way. He would find the guy who did it. He promised Leo as he stared at the grainy picture. He owed him that much. But he couldn't deny Boyd was good. He was a thief, and a good one at that. Probably one of the best. He was also anonymous which made his decision an even harder one. They needed someone like him on their team. But would Rhys ever forgive him? He wasn't sure.

"Marjorie," he called, and she entered his office shortly after. "What's on your calendar for the rest of the day?"

"A few things that can be pushed off, sir. What can I do?"

"Can you help me with something?" he asked.

"Of course, sir." She stepped further into the room.

"May take a while. Reroute all calls to voicemail, grab some tacks and string. Then meet me here in ten."

"Yes, sir," she smiled. "How many tacks, how much string?"

"A lot."

"Understood, I'll be back in ten."

"Thank you." He leaned back in his chair after she left staring at the police sketch Rhys had given of Boyd. "We're going to find you."

Almost exactly ten minutes later, Marjorie knocked on his door and entered with the requested items and two mugs of coffee.

"Excellent. Take my chair. You're going to help me find someone who doesn't want to be found," Kiter said.

"Ooh, this sounds fun." Marjorie set her gigantic mug of coffee down on his desk and sat in the faux leather chair.

"We're going to look up addresses of local pubs where these incidents have been reported," he indicated the fifty or so files he had printed from the police database. "Then use the pins and string to mark them on the map behind me."

"And the purpose of this little excursion?" She asked sipping the coffee in her mug.

"Two-fold, one a... friend of mine was robbed last night and I want to find his stuff, and secondly... well, we might have a new recruit." Kiter stated.

Marjorie's eyes widened. "And this *friend* who was robbed? Could he be your plus one?"

"Already has been and unfortunately may never be again." Kiter turned away from her all too knowing eyes.

"Now, could you look up these addresses and give me cross streets?" He opened the first file. "The Dancing Head near Westminster."

An hour later, they had all fifty tacks in the map of London and the string was weaved in and out and extended to notes pinned or taped to the wall with last name, date, and Boyd's pseudonym used in that con. The web was impressive.

"I gotta hand it to this boy, boss," Marjorie said. "He's good. I couldn't imagine sleeping with some of those guys."

"Money is money." Kiter shrugged, his eyes still focusing on the web.

"But what if it's not?" She offered.

He turned to look at her. "What do you mean?"

"What if he doesn't do all of these for money?"

"You have a theory?" He asked.

"Well, while you were finding the locations on the map, I did a little more digging. About fifteen of these guys he's conned have wound up in prison."

"For?"

"Child abuse, child pornography, pedophilia, the list is

long."

"You think he's some sort of vigilante?" Kiter asked.

"It's possible. According to two statements I was able to read, the police said they were given an anonymous tip from someone. The files were exactly where that person told them they would be. I don't know. What if he cons some of these guys not for money, but some because of who they are?"

"Rhys isn't a pedo," Kiter defended.

"No, of course not," she answered. "He falls into the money category. I'm just saying, maybe..."

"It's a good theory," Kiter turned to look at the map once more. The dots were fairly spread out for the London pubs. But one interested him above all the others. "This one, here." He pointed to the one farthest north in King's Lynn. "What's the story with this one?"

Marjorie shuffled some papers and pulled out the info as Kiter read off the note pinned to the wall with the words *McMasters, Falstaff,* and a date of five years ago.

"McMasters, Jacob. On the twenty-ninth of March five years ago, McMasters reported he was robbed overnight after bringing home a boy from the pub. He was arrested on child pornography and pedophilia charges. Currently serving out the last fifteen years of his sentence."

"Occupation?"

She shuffled the papers and scoffed. "Headmaster at a government funded orphanage."

"Where?"

"St. John's in King's Lynn."

"Five years ago. So if we're reading this correctly, and a lot of this is guess work, say this man was in the orphanage five years ago. That would put him at, what today? Twenty? Twenty-one? He would have been sixteen five years ago. And from the date, that was the first of Boyd's hits?"

"Yes, all the others started four years ago."

"And started here," he indicated London. "So with that info, we can," he moved around his desk and Marjorie scooted the chair away so he could type on the computer, "narrow down the age range to nineteen- to twenty-three-year-olds. And cross reference these names to the St. John's Orphanage for those years and we..." he waited until the computer dinged. "Got a hit. Boyd Falstaff," he pulled up the ID. "Twenty-one." Kiter glared at the picture. He was beautiful in a boyish way. And Kiter had placed him in the *Maybe* folder. Maybe he didn't know Rhys anymore. He would dissect that later.

"Last known address was the children's home. Nothing on the registrar." Marjorie took over the computer search while Kiter looked back at the map. "There's no record, sir."

"No, no of course not. He probably goes by a thousand different names." Kiter breathed still staring at the map. "We're looking at this all wrong. The men," he turned to look at her. "The men who were conned, the ones not arrested. Their statements say their money, keys, jewelry, anything quick and valuable was taken."

"Right, also looks like the last one said his safe was broken into."

"But was it just the cash," Kiter said.

"What do you mean?"

"Leo said his wallet was taken, the whole wallet, and looks like three hundred was used on his bank card. So, was it just the cash?"

"Leo?" She questioned.

"What?"

"You said *Leo said*, who are you talking about boss?"

He rubbed the back of his neck. "Nobody. I mean... the last victim, Rhys Campbell."

"But you called him Leo."

"Marjorie, could you pull up the files on the other victims please?"

Her smirk irritated him. "Sure thing. What are we looking for?"

"Did he take the other bank cards? If so, find the statements showing the transactions."

It took another thirty minutes to get all the statements up and reviewed. But as they found the bank machine withdrawal on each statement, a pattern emerged. The location of the ATM was the same. Just off Camden High Street. Looking up at the map, Camden had a very low concentration of pubs Boyd was known to have worked.

"Marge, get on the phone and call up all the pubs in this area. See if they recently hired someone matching Boyd's description. Be discreet and tell me as soon as you have something. I'll be on my mobile."

"On it," she said grabbing his desk phone and dialing.

He left his office hearing Marjorie speaking to the first pub.

Chapter Four

Leo opened the door to his flat with a harsh sigh. It had been an interesting day, to say the least. First, the realization he had been robbed by the man he brought home, then, hours at the police station, finally, lunch with Callum and an acceptance of a new job. The transfer papers were already on his chief's desk for signing in the morning. He was able to get a couple hundred pounds out of his savings account to survive the next few days while the shitshow died down. Was he such an easy mark? Had he given off the desperation he felt? Was that why Boyd or whatever his real name was had picked him?

Sitting on his couch, he thanked his lucky stars his television was so old and not worth anything. His eyes also traveled to his father's military medals hanging below the Katana. At least he was nice enough not to take those. It was all he had left of his father and his Samurai sword was his pride and joy.

Leaning his head back on the sofa, he closed his eyes. He wanted to sleep for a week. He fortunately was able to get another prescription filled for his Vicodin and took a dose just a bit ago. But his stomach growled. Opening his eyes, he took his phone and ordered a pizza. He usually did Thai or something equally delicious and vegetarian, but the thought of crispy crust, melty cheese, and an over abundance of sauce was too much of a siren call to resist. He thought about being somewhat healthy and getting cauliflower crust but instead treated himself to the real thing.

As he waited for his pizza, he turned on the television and flicked through the channels. There was nothing on. Settling on a rerun of an old cop drama, Rhys stretched his long legs out in front of him. He couldn't honestly believe everything that happened that day. It felt like a year ago he met the kid at the pub not just twenty-four hours ago. He shook his head and glanced down at his wrist only to realize his watch was gone. Heaving a heavy sigh, he refused to continue his pity party.

The doorbell's shrill ring echoed throughout the flat. Surprised the pizza got there so fast, he stood and grabbed a twenty and a five from his makeshift wallet on the counter. Hurrying to the door as the delivery driver knocked, Rhys called out. "Coming, yeah, sorry. You're early. I didn't expect—" he froze mid sentence when he opened the door to, not a pimply faced kid holding a pizza box, but the striking face of his old love, Sommerset Kiter.

"Sorry," Kiter looked uncomfortable. "Are you expecting someone?"

"What the hell are you doing here?" Rhys demanded.

"Can I come in?"

"No," Leo replied crossing his arms over his chest. Kiter deflated. "How do you know where I live?"

Kiter licked his lips, a tell he always had even as kids to show he was nervous. "I've always known."

"You stalk me?" Leo demanded.

"No no, nothing like that, just..." he looked away. "I'm sorry. I... I wanted to say..." he heaved a sigh that Leo felt down to his bones. "I am sorry," Kiter looked up at him. Leo was always helpless staring into those eyes and seeing the small wrinkles at the corners made it even harder to keep his emotions in check. Leo knew growing up Kiter would be a handsome man, and he wasn't wrong.

"Sorry? For what?" Leo gathered himself enough to ask.

"For everything. Please, can we not do this out here? Could I take us to dinner? I heard about what happened."

"I'm not a charity case, Scorpio," Leo spat. "How the hell did you know about any of it?"

"It's a long story. Look, come out to dinner with me. Let's talk?"

"No," Leo stated squaring up and standing with his feet apart and arms still crossed. He hoped he looked more intimidating than he felt.

Kiter looked away. "I know you hate me."

Leo's heart lurched. "I don't hate you. I should and I hate that I don't. But I don't hate you. You have to mean something to someone in order to hate them. And you mean nothing to me."

Leo watched as Kiter swallowed, his Adam's Apple bobbing in his throat. But Sommerset took a deep breath and pulled something out of his pocket.

"I realize how shitty of a person I am and know how horrible what I did to you was. I finally realized how much it hurt you and how badly I handled the situation with Geoff and you. I realized what I did to you was the worst betrayal. I ruined our future. I caused you to hate me and there's nothing I can do to make it up to you. I realized today how selfish I was and am. I wanted to say I am sorry.

"I wanted to tell you how much you meant and still mean to me. I never stopped loving you, Rhys and I know beyond a shadow of a doubt I deserve nothing from you, so I do not ask for your forgiveness, because I don't deserve it. But before I leave today and walk out of your life forever, just please know I love you and I am so very sorry for what I did to you and to us. I heard about what happened to you and I did some research. I found this at a pawn shop in Camden. I remembered how much it meant to you. I wanted to give it to you... again, I guess."

Leo looked down to see what was in Kiter's hand and gasped when he saw his watch. "How did you?" He didn't finish his question only snatched it and flipped it over, seeing the inscription.

LEO

Element: FIRE

Leader, Passionate, Dynamic

Ad astra per aspera.

His thumb brushed the Zodiac team's motto, *Through adversity to the stars.* The words swam as tears gathered in his eyes.

"I didn't think I'd ever see this again."

"I know," Kiter shrugged. "I'm glad you have it, now." Leo

wrapped his wrist with the watch band finally feeling whole again.

He looked up and locking eyes with Kiter again he continued, "I can't go out to dinner with you." Kiter closed his eyes briefly and nodded. "But I can thank you for finding this and coming to the realization. Thank you for your apology. It's been a long time coming but it is accepted."

Kiter swallowed hard. "Thank you," he said softly. They stared at each other for a long moment, the world narrowing to Kiter's eyes. Leo didn't want to look away. All the history. All the love they shared. Their families loved each other. Their parents accepted them as partners, encouraged it even. Rhys always thought they'd be married by then. He had his whole life with Kiter planned when he was twenty-two. But staring into the eyes of the forty-two-year-old man in front of him, the warmth and love he always felt for him, twisted in his stomach and his heart clenched.

"I've always loved you, you know," Rhys finally said. Kiter nodded and licked his lip. A shimmer of tears in his eyes. "Just tell me one thing? Why? Just tell me why?"

Kiter's face contorted in pain and his hand clenched at his side. He opened his mouth as if to speak and ran his tongue across the back of his teeth. "I wish I knew." He finally admitted. "I wish I knew, Rhys. Rebellion? Stagnation? Hurt? I don't know. Geoff... he was there. He wanted me. He was fresh and young and made me feel wanted and needed. You had your military career. You were deployed. I hadn't felt like you *needed* me in a very long time. It was my fault. I should have rejected him but maybe it was a way for me to feel wanted again. Every time I close my eyes, I see your face. The face you made when you walked in. That happiness to be home and see me then the confusion, then the realization, then the pain, and finally the anger. I think about it all the time. I wish I knew why. I wish I could give you the answer you deserve to have. But I don't know. And I'm sorry for that."

"Was I not enough for you?" Leo asked his words catching on the lump in his throat.

Kiter stepped forward but seemed to think better of it. "Of course you were. Rhys, I've loved you since I was fourteen. My choice had nothing to do with you. And all to do with how stupid I was."

Taking a deep breath, Leo's eyes fell to Kiter's wrist where his watch lay wrapped around him. "Thank you. Thank you for giving me that answer."

"I would give you anything, you know that."

Leo nodded and was about to speak when another voice interrupted him. "Ehm... I have a pizza for Rhys Campbell?"

They turned to see the pizza delivery kid holding the warmer.

"Yeah, that's me," Leo wiped his face and handed the kid the money. "Keep the change."

"Cheers, mate," he said and left the hallway. Leo stood awkwardly holding the pizza box while waiting to know what Kiter would do next.

"I'll — ehm — let you eat. Get out of your hair," Sommerset said.

"Yeah, yeah, thanks." Kiter nodded and turned away, but Leo needed to see him one more time. "Hey, S—S—Somm," he hadn't said that name in nearly twenty years and it got caught in his throat. Kiter froze then turned slowly. "Thank you."

His eyes lighting with hope, Sommerset flashed a brief tight smile. "Always, Rhys." With that, Leo watched as Kiter walked down the hallway to the elevators and disappeared from sight.

Chapter Five

Kiter fought to not look back at Rhys as he turned the corner to the elevators in the apartment building. He wasn't sure what he feared the most, that Rhys wouldn't be watching him… or that he would be.

At least he was able to return his watch. All of the members of the Zodiacs received one when they retired or were discharged. Each watch had an inscription based on their call sign which was their Zodiacs. It was a precious gift to all of them. Kiter looked down at his own watch and smiled softly. But his reminiscing was cut short by his phone ringing. Answering Marjorie's call, he pressed it to his ear.

"What have you found?"

"Boyd Falstaff, under the name Anders is currently working tonight at the gay bar Sir Wines a Lot in South Hampstead just off A41," Marjorie said.

"Send me the address."

"Done."

"And can you get a hotel room near there and call Callum. We'll use him in this situation."

"On it. Meet you there in an hour." Marjorie hung up and Kiter's elevator car dinged. He hoped he was doing the right thing... But more importantly, he hoped Rhys would forgive him for not telling him about his involvement in the new team and the recruitment of the man who violated Rhys's trust in the most intimate way possible.

Kiter watched Callum O'Grady adjust the pen mic in his lapel pocket as Marjorie tested the device. If things got heated between Callum and Boyd, they didn't want their plan to be discovered if he felt an under-the-shirt wire. They opted for the newer tech of Bluetooth enabled camera and mic. It connected to the device in Marjorie's hand up to fifty feet away and as they would be following Callum's car if all went as planned, they would always be in range. The gay bar was just across the street from the hotel room and the window overlooked the upscale wine bar.

Callum was young, handsome, and looked wealthy, at least with the Armani shoes, £3000 watch on his wrist, and £90 haircut. He was also a university recruit into the spy craft when he went to college in Scotland. Callum knew what he was doing, and the fact he was gay helped them in that situation. He was a perfect honey trap for Boyd.

"You sure about this, boss?" Callum asked shrugging into his suit jacket. "I mean, I get wanting to get even with what he did to Leo, but recruiting him? I doubt Leo will like having to work with the guy who stole from him, let alone slept with him."

Kiter winced. He thought that too. "I'm sure," he went on ignoring Marjorie's look. "The kid has skills we need on the team. He cracked Leo's wall safe in under three minutes. It's an Am Vault TL-30, he's good. And yeah, I do want to get back at him for putting Leo through that, but his skills cool that flame. Even still, mess with him a little." He winked.

Callum chuckled as he grabbed his tie and proceeded to tie a perfect Windsor. Marjorie made a sound in her throat and Callum stopped. "What?" He questioned.

She glanced back at Kiter. "You said Boyd's marks are usually depressed or sad, right?"

Kiter nodded. She pulled Callum's tie so it looked like he had loosened it, popped the top button of the collar, untucked one side of the shirt, pull off the suit jacket, rolled up his sleeves to the elbow, crumpled the suit jacket in her hands to wrinkle it, slung it over his arm, then ran her fingers through Callum's dark hair releasing the gel holding it and allowing it to look like he had run his fingers through it many times throughout the day. In short, she took Callum's pristine ensemble and created a bloody shamble.

She then took her bag of supplies and found the tweezers. "This'll hurt, sorry." She said to Callum.

"What?" He questioned then yelped when she stuck the tweezers into this nose and yanked some nose hair out. "Ow, shite, Marge, that hurt!" His eyes instantly watered and he rubbed the tip of his nose with his palm to ease the pain. His nose went red, and his eyes watered looking like he had been or was on the verge of crying.

"Sorry, tried to warn you," Marjorie put the tweezers back in her pouch. "Now you're ready."

With a final comm check, he headed out the door.

"Nice trick," Kiter said to Marjorie as she straightened the room.

She shrugged. "It makes the eyes shine as if he's cried."

"I noticed. Good job."

The sounds of the pub came to life over the mic and their attention went to the screen showing the pub from Callum's lapel. Scanning the room, he paused when he saw Boyd wiping a glass with a bar towel.

"Target acquired. Confirm?"

Marjorie looked at the camera and then the file folder with Boyd Falstaff's information.

"Affirmative, Frax, that's Baby Bear."

"Moving in position to engage, standby."

Callum walked to the bar and slid into one of the stools. Letting out a sigh, he ran his hands through his hair and grunted in frustration. "Idiot." He muttered to himself as part of the character he was playing. A young man, matching the picture of Boyd Falstaff looked over behind the bar.

"Hey handsome," he said slipping down the long bar to stand in front of Callum. "Tough day? What can I get you?"

"Cab make it a double pour. Nah, leave the bottle," Callum said.

Boyd's eyes widened and his brows rose. "Tough day?" He asked grabbing the bottle from behind the counter.

"You could say that."

"You're Irish?" Boyd grinned setting the glass down and taking out the bottle opener.

"I am."

"I like the accent." The cork gave a satisfying pop as it was pried loose. Boyd poured a healthy pour into the wine glass and leaned over the counter, his black mesh shirt tantalizing setting the glass in front of Callum, he placed the bottle next to the glass. "So tell me, what's going on? Gorgeous guy like you shouldn't have it tough."

"My ex-boyfriend just invited me to his wedding... to a woman," Callum said.

Boyd flinched. "That sucks. Was he in the closet?"

"Aye," Callum answered picking up the drink. "We used to fight about it all the time. And if that wasn't shitty enough, I got knocked out for best sales spot by the rookie. My head's just not in the game recently."

"Why's that?"

Callum took a large sip of his drink. "Imposter Syndrome? I don't know. When Dale left me, I don't know, it's like one minute I have my future planned out with a great guy, and the next..."

"You're getting a wedding invite from the guy you wanted to spend forever with," Boyd finished.

Callum let out a self-deprecating laugh and stared at him. "Sounds like you know from experience."

"Something like that."

Callum raised his glass to Boyd. "Well, here's to us. Two gorgeous men who have nothing figured out."

Callum drained his drink flashing the watch Boyd's way. The man's eyes widened.

"Hook's in," Kiter said as he watched Boyd's reaction through the camera.

"Look," Boyd began, pouring another drink for him. "You are gorgeous. You'll find someone new."

"I don't want anyone. Not for long term at least... not yet anyway. Besides, I'm basically married to my job. No friends. No family. Just me in my flat. I mean it's got a nice view, should for what I pay for it, but it's cold. Lonely."

"What's the view?"

"Hyde Park," Callum answered taking another drink.

Boyd froze. "Hyde Park?"

Callum waved him off, "sorry, forget I said anything."

"What are you doing way out here if you live there?" Boyd asked.

Callum looked around. "Gay bar?" He offered. "And I was driving for a bit after work. Trying to clear my head. Thought it might make me feel... I don't know, connected to people somehow? It's working, I mean, apart from you, but no offense, you're a bartender you're supposed to treat me like a friend."

"No, I don't," he winked.

"God, you're hot when you do that." Then Callum covered his mouth. "Shit, sorry. Ignore me. Red wine and whiskey always gets me. I have no filter. You probably have other customers."

"None as handsome," Boyd shrugged and topped off Callum's glass. "We've got a drag show tonight. Might be interesting for you to stick around."

"Nah, I should be getting back. I got to work tomorrow." Callum drained the wine in one long drink and promptly hiccuped. "Shite, sorry."

Kiter covered his smirk. He had seen Callum knock back two bottles with hardly any side effects but his ability to pretend was second to none.

After paying, Callum pulled out the keys for the Range Rover they had borrowed from MI6's impound lot. Boyd covered his hand. "Hey, you probably shouldn't drive in your condition."

"I'm fine," Callum waved him off.

"No, seriously. I don't feel right about letting you drive. Besides it could mean I get in trouble for serving you."

"You can finish the bottle," he offered to Boyd.

"How about I wrap it up and we finish it together? My shift is up in two minutes. I'll drive you home."

"I couldn't... I mean, you'd have no way home."

Boyd shrugged, a salacious grin crossing his lips. "Damn, have to spend the night with the hot as hell sales bloke... whatever would we do to pass the time?"

Callum said nothing for a moment, then, he let Boyd have the keys. "Okay."

"Good," Boyd grinned. "Tan, I'm out," he called to who Kiter assumed was the other bartender.

Wiping his hands on the bar rag, Boyd took the keys and met Callum on the other side of the bar.

Boyd drove the Range Rover making small talk while Kiter drove with Marjorie a few cars behind, staying within range of the Bluetooth. They had commandeered a flat in The Towers to use for their sting operation and Callum directed Boyd where to go.

Kiter's phone buzzed and Marjorie took it, checking the text.

"Text from Lester. Wanted to know the name of your plus one for the party next week," she announced reading the message.

Kiter shook his head. "Doesn't that man have his own wife and love life? Why is he so fixated on mine?"

She shrugged. "Wants to be supportive?"

"Not the way to do it."

Silence filled the car as they continued to drive. The only sound was Callum's and Boyd's voices coming from the speakers speaking of nothing important. After a while, Marjorie spoke again.

"So... Leo, huh?"

Kiter's grip on the steering wheel increased, the leather groaning under the pressure.

"What about him?"

"Come on, boss. After everything we've been through together? You're not going to tell me? Are you two back together?" She asked.

"I should never have revealed that to you. It was a drunken evening and I apologize for breaking professionalism," Kiter replied.

"Pish posh," she waved him off. "I was just as drunk. You know about my failed relationships. But you two... there's something more there. I can feel it."

"Can you? You've never met the man."

"I don't need to," she shrugged. "I could hear it in your voice."

"Look, Marge, I appreciate you being interested in my love life, but Leo and I are just... well... I don't know what we are. But I hope I can say friends."

"Well, you'll have to prove to him you've changed. He does know about this whole thing right?"

Kiter's lips pressed together.

"Sommerset, you have told him about your involvement in The Charing Cross Boys, right?" she pressed.

"The right time hasn't presented itself."

"He's transferring in three days! You can't spring it on him."

"I think I know him better than you do, Marjorie."

"You don't know human nature, boss. If you think he'll be okay with this, think again."

Kiter said nothing, He couldn't. He knew she was right. He had to tell Rhys soon but how and when? Was he a coward for not wanting to tell him and allowing him to find out organically? He knew that answer. But he had little time to think more about it, as they pulled in the car park for The Towers. From their spot in the shadows, Kiter and Marjorie watched as Boyd helped Callum out of the car. Cal was acting a little drunk and allowed Boyd to lift his wallet from his pocket as he steadied him. Callum turned them both trapping Boyd against the car. He leaned down and kissed him, their hands exploring each other's bodies. Boyd rubbed up against him like a cat, letting out a purr too.

Callum pulled back and pressed his forehead against Boyd's. "I've been wanting to kiss you since I first saw you."

"Then let's get inside and do more than just kiss," Boyd replied.

Callum caressed his cheek and Kiter and Marjorie leaned forward. "When did he get the watch?" Marjorie asked. "Did you see him lift the watch?"

Kiter shook his head. "He's good."

They waited until Callum and Boyd were in the elevator to get out of the car. Walking together, Marjorie waited to speak until Kiter pushed the call button for the elevator car.

"Boss, I'm sorry. I shouldn't have pried into your personal life. I just worry about you. I want you happy. That's all."

"It's fine, Marge," he answered. "I get it. I don't have an answer for Leo's and my relationship, but I hope one day you can see me happy."

She smiled softly and let the subject drop. "So how do you want to play this?"

"Well, Boyd has two options," Kiter began as the elevator dinged. They got into the car and pushed the button for the twelfth floor. "He can join us, or he can be a guest of Her Majesty. I think I know which one he'll choose."

"Hope you're right. His skills could help the team," she said.

The elevator arrived and they stepped off, walking down the hall to the flat.

With no warning knock, they opened the door and walked in. Boyd looked up from where he had just picked the lock on the desk. Callum was no where to be seen.

"Who are you?" Boyd demanded. "What do you want? How did you get in here?"

"Boyd Falstaff, we need to speak with you," Kiter said.

"How do you...?" He began but the bathroom door opened, and Callum walked out. Seeing Kiter and Marjorie, he stopped in the bedroom doorway and crossed his arms.

"Took you long enough, boss," he said.

"Boss?" Boyd questioned.

"You didn't have to kiss him," Kiter replied.

"He hadn't gotten my watch yet. Had to give him a chance," Callum answered.

"What...?" Boyd looked between all three of them, then deflated. "You're a cop."

Callum shrugged. "Not exactly."

"Then what is this?" Boyd demanded.

"Take a seat, Mr. Falstaff," Kiter said. Boyd crossed his arms over his chest but said nothing. "Very well, if you want to do it this way." Kiter motioned with his head to Callum who took up his stance in front of the front door preventing Boyd from running.

Kiter sat on one of the wingback chairs and crossed his ankle over his knee... and waited. It took Boyd less than thirty seconds for the nervous energy building in him to explode.

"Look, I'll give it all back."

Kiter raised an eyebrow. "All?"

"I've got the watch here," he pulled it out of his pocket. "And your wallet and keys. I didn't mean anything by it."

"No?" Kiter questioned.

"A guy's gotta eat, right?" He tried. "And I mean, the sex, that's just a bonus. It's not like I'm in it for the money. I'm not a sex worker... not that there's anything wrong with that! It's just not for me... I mean... ehum..." The poor guy was floundering. Kiter threw him a lifeline.

"I want you to work for us," Kiter said. Boyd stopped and stared. He reminded Kiter of a young deer.

"You... what?"

"I run a team of special elites. Each man and woman has

special skills. Yours are unique. I want you on our team."

Boyd stared then looked from one to the other quickly. "Work for you? Doing what? I'm no cop."

"But you have delivered justice before, no?" Kiter questioned. Boyd's brow furrowed. "McMasters? Smythe? Manson? Hunter? All convicted of heinous crimes because of an anonymous tip and reported to the police they were robbed by someone they took home. Tell me, did you sleep with them too? Or just go and find their stash in order to report them?"

"I never let any of those disgusting monsters touch me. I only ever sleep with the men I actually find attractive. The others, sure I fool around with them, get them to trust me. But they never touched me. It was a game. Their fantasy. I never let it happen. I know what I am doing."

"Of course," Kiter answered, though his stomach tightened with the idea he had found Leo attractive enough to actually sleep with him.

"You know a lot about me," Boyd said turning to gaze out the window at Hyde Park.

"We do, Falstaff."

"Boyd," he corrected. "I don't go by that name."

"Boyd, it is then." Kiter stood and headed over to him. "Listen, son, I'll not beat around the bush here, we need you on our team. I need your skills. You would be a valued member of an elite squad."

"I become a spook, or I go to jail, is that it?" He looked over at him.

"It's not that simple," Kiter answered.

"Sure it is. You either get me to turn tricks for you, or Billy Bobblehead does in Belmarsh Prison."

"There are no tricks to turn. We're not looking for your sexual skills. We need your cat burglar abilities, a hacker, someone who is an expert on lock picking, safe cracking, and technology."

After a beat, Boyd turned fully to Kiter and offered his wrists. "I'd rather try my hand in prison. Who knows, might pick up a few new tricks."

They were silent for a long moment and Kiter sighed. Then, Callum stepped forward. "You feel invisible. You think no one sees you so you don't exist. You believe you're not worth anything because your abuser told you you weren't. They said you would never amount to anything and after a suitable time of rebellion, you began to believe them because they were the only ones who cared about you, and they wouldn't lie to you. But let me tell you something, Boyd, you are someone special. I see you but they didn't, Boyd. They didn't care about you. Everything they told you was a lie. You *are* worth it. You're worth everything. They hurt you. They didn't care about you. You fought back the only way you knew how, and you prevented him from hurting others. We're giving you another chance to stop people like your abuser, and hundreds, thousands, like them.

"Speaking from personal experience, this team is formed from another who broke up two sex trafficking rings. Those young men and women, just like you, have a life to live now. And they have a choice just as you do. Do I cower from the cowards who hurt me and made me like this? Or, do I stand tall? Do I prove to myself *and* them, they have no hold on me? I am *not* who they wanted to create. I am me. The person *I* want to be. Is that person in prison for a decade or more with only a glimmer of hope they won't have to perform certain acts on and for others as before? In that scenario, nothing changes and you're still that abused, scared, little boy? Or is that person a valued member of a team? One respected by their peers using the skills honed and mastered over the years? Standing up to evil, adversity, and through the pain, helping others the way you wanted to be helped but never were? The choice is yours to make. But one way or another, you will have to make it. So, Boyd Falstaff, what'll it be? Will you allow your abuser to win? Or will you stand up for yourself and say; here I am, I am me whether you like it or not. There's nothing you can do about it?"

Kiter waited to hear Boyd's answer. He knew how difficult it was for Callum to speak those words drawing from personal experience to convince the younger man. He hoped his friend, the man he looked at like a younger brother, felt the love both he and Marjorie had for him. Kiter was the one who pulled Callum out of the sex trafficking ring he had been forced into. He was the one who gave Callum new life, a new hope, and Kiter specifically remembered telling a twenty-two-year-old Callum some of those same words he just spoke, five years ago. Not turning to look at the man he mentored, he watched Boyd. The much younger man stared at Callum, the wheels in his head turning. He was debating, Kiter could tell.

Finally, Boyd opened his mouth and spoke low. "Do I get to pick my own code name? Or will we have stupid ones like 007 or something?"

Kiter chuckled. "So long as it's tasteful, you can pick your own."

"Good," he looked at Kiter. "What's yours?"

"I only use it in the field. But it's Scorpio."

"Badass," Boyd said. Then, he turned to Callum. "What's yours?"

Callum said nothing for a while before answering. "Fraxinus."

"The Ash tree?" Boyd questioned. At Callum's and Kiter's raised eyebrows, he shrugged. "Catholic orphanage for a couple years before St. John's became a ward of the state. Latin isn't hard. I liked Botany and had a knack for Latin."

"Do you know what the Ash Tree represents?" Callum asked.

"It means *spear* in Latin so I would assume... fighting?"

"It's the symbol for the protection of children," Callum said.

Boyd and Callum locked eyes for a long moment. "You were... abused."

"I was trafficked as a sex slave when I was twenty-one. I was in for six months before Kiter got me out."

Boyd closed his eyes for a moment then took a deep breath. When he opened his eyes they were much less haunted. And stronger as he nodded once to Callum then turned to Kiter.

"When do I start?"

Chapter Six

Leo straightened his tie again for the sixth time in as many minutes. He had arrived at the address given to him by Special Agent O'Grady thirty minutes ago and after rigorous security checks, he had been escorted up to the fifth floor and told to wait. That was ten minutes ago, and he was starting to worry everything was a big con... again. His watch still on his wrist, began to burn as if a reminder of his weekend stupidity.

The sound of a door opening pulled him back to reality. A woman, perhaps in her fifties if Leo had to guess walked out.

"So sorry to keep you waiting," she said with a friendly smile as she walked over to him. "I'm Marjorie. You must be Rhys Campbell?"

"Aye," he stood and took her hand. "Please call me Leo. Rhys is as foreign to me as my middle name."

"Of course, Angus," she winked using his middle name.

He cringed but kept a friendly smile on his face. "I opened myself up for that one, eh?"

She laughed. "I always like to play with the new recruits. Make them laugh. I find it puts them at ease. Especially when the surroundings are so unfamiliar." She headed over to the desk and pulled out a file. "I am the administrator for the Boss and the Team. Anything you need, you let me know. We're happy to have you on board. There are just two documents to go over and I'll need your signature before I can escort you back to the team."

"Not a problem. There's more on the team now?" He questioned. "It's just, last time I spoke with Agent O'Grady he said it was just the two of us so far."

A look clouded her face as she looked down at the file and pulled out paperclipped sheets. "Yes, Callum and our boss recruited one other over the weekend."

"Grand, I'm looking forward to meeting them."

"Yes, I know you are," she still didn't look up at him. "Now," she placed the paperclipped sheets on a clipboard and showed it to him. "This is the official paperwork. Just check the salary and name is correct. Then sign here and initial there." He did. "And this one," she flipped the page. "Is the standard company NDA. But this right here is unique to our team. Please review at your leisure and sign here."

Leo reviewed the paperwork. There as nothing unusual about the NDA, except for the section pertaining to the team. "This here. What does it mean?" He asked pointing to the second paragraph.

"All agents are required to maintain the confidentiality of their fellow agents, superiors, technology, and locations.

Failure to do so will result in disciplinary action up to and including *Burn Notice?*"

"It means anyone who reveals the identities of their team or the technology and secret locations to anyone not on the team will be removed," she explained nonchalantly as she clicked around on the computer. "Permanently."

"I see," he replied.

"Good, and as this team will be participating in unsanctioned missions, it is vital for the sustainability of the program that all personal and safe houses be maintained under the strictest of secrecy."

"I'm sorry... *un*sanctioned?" Rhys questioned.

"Yes."

"What does that mean exactly?"

"It gives us the ability to do what needs to be done," Callum's voice from the doorway surprised him. He turned and Callum walked over to him. "But mainly it means if we get caught, we're on our own."

"You didn't mention that at lunch," Leo said.

"That's because it's not something I want aired in public," Callum walked over. "You still in?"

"Don't have much choice, do I?"

"There's always a choice, Leo," Callum said. "So what'll it be?"

With a sigh, Leo signed his name. "What the hell, I've come this far."

Callum grinned and patted him on the back. "That's the spirit. Come meet our other recruit."

Leo handed Marjorie the paperwork trying to discern the look on her face as she gave Callum a stern expression. But he followed Callum through the door, down the hall, and into a boardroom where two other men waited. The second he was through the door, his stomach plummeted.

"What the hell is going on?" He demanded locking eyes with Kiter.

"Rhys, hear me out," Kiter tried, hands raised in supplication.

"What the hell are you doing here?" Leo demanded. "Are you trying to be in every aspect of my life now? You can't have me in bed, so you have to have me work for you?"

"Woah, TMI, mate, I don't want to know about that. It'll be tough enough to know you've slept with fifty percent of the guys on the team."

That voice. Leo couldn't believe it. He was so focused on Kiter that he had ignored the other man in the room. And when Boyd walked over to Kiter, the same saucy smile and swing in his hips as the night he had been duped, it was too much.

"Oh hell no, what the hell, Kiter?"

"We all need to take a breath. Agent Boyd is here as a new recruit just like you."

"New... is this a joke? This man stole from me. By rights I should arrest him!" Leo shouted.

"Rhys," Kiter tried.

"Look mate, it was nothing personal. I'm glad you got your watch back. I can return... some of the stuff I took. I still have your wallet and I can get you some of the money back."

"I don't want your money!" Leo's anger burst forth. "I want to know what the hell a common criminal is doing here!"

"I can't apologize enough for what I did. It wasn't personal. I actually really liked you. I enjoyed our time together.

It's just habit, okay?" Boyd continued. "I didn't touch anything I knew was personally valuable. I know the medals you had meant something, I have one from my granddad and the sword, that could have made me a lot of money, but you had told me how much it meant to you, so I left it alone."

"I'm supposed to be grateful you only took *some* of my stuff?"

"I... I don't know what to say, okay? I'm sorry." Boyd looked down and for a moment through his hatred, embarrassment, and hurt, Rhys saw the true remorse in his eyes. "I did really like you. I wouldn't mind a do over. If you're game."

"That won't be happening," Kiter stated, his back straight and his posture ready to pounce.

"Oh so you don't want me to have a personal life now, too?" Leo demanded. "You don't own me, Sommerset. You don't rule my life. What are you even doing here?"

"I'm not trying to rule anything. You are your own man. There is a no fraternization clause for those coming to the team as single men. We have a couple on board that have been a couple for a while so they will not be affected by it."

"Fraternization? You're quoting paperwork now?"

"I..."

"Oh shite, you're the boss, aren't you?" Leo questioned. Kiter took a breath and a moment, but Leo had his answer. He looked away and saw Callum standing stoically near the door. "Did *he* recruit me, or did you? You claimed to be friends with someone I worked with."

"I didn't lie to you," Callum said. "But I didn't tell you everything."

"A lie by omission is still a lie." Leo looked around the room, taking in one after the other. "You all lied to me. You all took me for a fool. You stole from me," he looked at Boyd. "You lied to me about your true intentions," he looked at Callum. "And you... you can't tell me the truth if your life depended on it." He stared holes into Kiter. "How am I supposed to trust any of you?" After a moment, he looked back at Callum. "Thank you for the opportunity, Agent O'Grady, but I will not be continuing in this position or with this team. Please have my paperwork transferred back to Scotland Yard as soon as possible. I understand I'm still obligated to keep the terms of the NDA and I will." With that, Leo walked out of the room with a twist of his heart and knot in his stomach.

"That could have gone better," Marjorie's voice came from the door. The team turned to look at her as she entered the room a few moments after Rhys left. "I told you you should have told him, boss."

Kiter sighed. "I didn't know how to."

"So... what's the story?" Boyd asked. "You guys obviously have history."

"None of your business," Kiter answered.

"I think it is, boss," Callum agreed. "You didn't tell me you two were exes. Had I known the whole story, I would never have recruited him."

"That's not your choice, Callum," Kiter said. "You recruit who I tell you to."

"That's not how this is going to go, boss," Callum stated and sat down at the table. "Talk to us."

Boyd sat next to him, and they both looked at Kiter expectantly. Kiter stared at the three of them, his resolve breaking.

"Rhys Campbell and I have known each other since we were fourteen. We were friends, then we were more than, then we broke up."

"Why?" Boyd asked.

"That's not important."

"Boss cheated on him." Marjorie offered. Kiter stared daggers at her. "What? That's what happened, isn't it?"

"That's not important," Kiter said again. "He was recruited into the SRR due to his military career. The team he was assigned to was mine. The Zodiacs. Hence why his name is Leo and mine is Scorpio. He didn't appreciate seeing me again after all those years, but he knew he was good, and we needed him on our team. I had nothing to do with him joining my team, it was as much a surprise to me as it was to him. The military didn't know our history. He was a valued member of our team and fast became my second in command, until he was injured. He was medically discharged and given that watch." Kiter looked down at his and pulled it off, handing it to Marjorie. "Everyone in my team got one. Their Zodiac, along with their element, personality traits, and our motto."

"Scorpio," Boyd read on the watch when Marjorie handed it to him. "Water. Intelligent, Intuitive, Focused. *Ad astra per aspera*. Through adversity to the stars."

"Yes, the Zodiacs."

"And the samurai sword?" Boyd asked passing the watch to Callum.

"Rhys speaks five languages, English, French, Russian,

Japanese, and Urdu. He has possible Mandarin, Spanish, and Portuguese. He's boots on the ground for any whisper of an event. He spent three years in Japan when his father was stationed Okinawa. He learned Jujitsu, and studied Kendo, the way of the sword. Those medals you mentioned were of his father who was KIA."

"KIA?" Boyd asked.

"Killed in Action," Callum explained.

Boyd's face went white, and he closed his eyes for a long moment. "Do you really think he's not going to come back?"

"When Rhys makes up his mind, there's no changing it. Obstinance, a trait of the Leo," Kiter explained.

"This sucks," Boyd grunted and leaned back in his chair.

"Indeed, but nevertheless, we have to move on. Callum, how are we with Hesler and Darius?"

"Both interested, going to bring them in when they return from their vacation, end of the week," Callum said.

"Good, let's keep an eye open for another recruit soon. We have an op in a couple months."

"Speaking of," Marjorie looked down at her smartwatch. "Commander Lester is in the lobby wanting to speak to you."

Kiter huffed. "Not the time."

"He'll probably want an answer to that question," Marjorie said.

"What question?" Boyd piped up suddenly interested.

Kiter looked between them. "Either of you fancy being my date to a party?"

"Party?" Callum questioned.

"It's a christening so to speak of our team. Commander Lester, my boss, wants me to bring a boyfriend to make the more… straitlaced members of Parliament squirm."

"Well, hell, I've slept with Leo, made out with Callum, might as well, be your date to make all the old farts jealous," Boyd offered.

"Not helping, Boyd," Callum stated.

"I'm just saying, I'm here for you, boss," Boyd said.

"Only if you call me Daddy the entire time," Kiter was happy to find the humor in the situation. Even if he didn't feel like it was all that funny.

"Ooh, I can do that, Daddy," Boyd winked making them all laugh.

Kiter sighed and shook his head. "No, I can't do that to you. I'll be going alone."

"Awe, no fair," Boyd complained.

"I'll go greet him, boss," Marjorie said.

"No, I'll go," he answered. "Gotta face the man sooner or later. Callum, why don't you take Boyd downstairs to the shooting range. I assume you've never fired a gun before?" He looked at Boyd.

"You'd assume correctly," Boyd replied. "I can't shoot a gun."

"You have fingers, don't you?" Callum questioned. "You can shoot a gun."

Boyd chewed on his lip. "Okay. I'll try."

Kiter led the way out of the boardroom and waved goodbye as Callum took Boyd down a back stair to the shooting range in the basement. Kiter and Marjorie continued to the lobby of their offices and greeted Lester.

"Didn't want to interrupt. Thought I could meet the new recruits." Lester said once they had greeted each other.

"Unfortunately, sir there's been a delay in one of our recruits. But I fully intend to have him here or replaced before the op."

Lester nodded slowly. "Hmm," he said. "All right. And the other?"

"The other is currently being shown the ropes by O'Grady. He's a civilian so there are several things he needs to learn."

"You took my advice. I like that."

"It was sound advice, sir, and it made me see that there are other avenues to go through if things get tied up."

"Good," Lester smiled. "Well, I am excited to know you've accepted the invitation to the party. We do need the name of your plus one for table placement and nametags."

"Unfortunately, sir, it looks like it'll just be me, myself, and I this time around."

Lester's face grew confused. "Oh, no, that will not do. That won't do at all. You must have someone there."

"Why is it so important, sir?"

"Well, I mean, I guess... It's all about image and for those stuffies to see you how you need to be seen, you need to show them you're not intimidated by their 15th century ideology. It's for the good of the team." Lester extended his hand. "Have someone picked by Friday and send me a text with his name."

Kiter shook his boss' hand, holding in his reaction. Lester left the area and Marjorie turned to him. "What are you going to do?"

"I don't know. I really don't know." As he said that, his phone rang. Pulling it out of his pocket, he chuckled, then when he answered. "Well well, impeccable timing."

"Is it? How so?" Geoff's voice came from the other end of the call.

"Know any single gay men available on Saturday night for a party?"

"Is that some sort of euphemism?" Geoff questioned.

"I wish it were."

"All right... well... not sure, but I think Peter and I can put our heads together to figure something out. What's going on?"

Kiter went into his office and shut the door. Groaning as he sat in his faux leather chair, he leaned his head back and closed his eyes. He told Geoff all about Lester's demands and how he couldn't just materialize someone to go with him, let alone feel comfortable enough with him to show the sort of PDA Lester was expecting. All without revealing the true names and nature of work. Geoff may be a good friend and retired Lieutenant Colonel of the SRR but he wasn't involved in the Charing Cross Boys.

"Shite, if I wasn't so banged up, I'd go with you," Geoff said.

"I don't think Peter would appreciate that," Kiter answered.

"True," Geoff paused. "He told me you told him about being my teacher at Sandringham. How we met."

"It came out," Kiter explained. "I didn't realize you had told him we slept together. He didn't like me all that much afterwards."

"I'm sorry if it made you uncomfortable, talking about it, I mean," Geoff said.

"No, it didn't make me uncomfortable, Geoff," Kiter answered. "But moving on, if you or Peter know of anyone who would be interested, give me a call."

"Actually," Geoff's voice took on that all too familiar *thinking* tone. "I called to invite you over for dinner tonight. Peter and I are cooking and wanted to invite the team. Humail can't make it on account of it being Eid al-Adha, but the rest of team is free. You're my last call."

"So happy to be so high on the priority list, there," Kiter chuckled.

"Had to wait until Peter went out to the off license."

"You did tell him you're inviting me, right?"

"Yes, yes, I promise. He's fine. He knows whose bed I sleep in at night. He has nothing to worry about," Geoff answered. "So, you coming?"

"Happily, so long as your boyfriend doesn't try to kill me."

"He wouldn't dare. He likes sex too much to risk me cutting him off."

Kiter chuckled again. "Good, what time?"

"2100?"

"I'll be there. What can I bring?"

"Surprise me."

"Wine it is."

"Exactly what I was hoping for," Geoff said. "See you soon."

After they hung up, Kiter glanced at the clock to see it was nearly four in the afternoon. Calling it a day, he logged out of his computer and headed for his door.

"I'm on my mobile if I'm needed, Marjorie," he called to her.

"Have a good evening," she answered.

Chapter Seven

Knocking on Geoff's townhouse door a little before 2100, Kiter wasn't surprised when Faust, Geoff's butler answered the door with a polite smile.

"Do you remember me, Faust?" He teased.

"Of course I do, Colonel," the elderly gentleman answered with a slight bow. "Though it has been a long time."

"It has indeed. How have you been?" Kiter asked offering him the bag containing the three bottles of wine as he stepped over the threshold.

"I'm happy his lordship is home safe and sound. He mentioned you helped in that scenario, sir. Thank you."

"It was all Captain Carlisle's doing. I was just along for the ride."

"Liar," he heard Geoff's voice from the doorway of the library where Geoff always welcomed his guests. "Peter's plan yes, but you helped implement it. Got the team together."

Kiter grinned at his friend. The thirty-five-year-old still had his dark black hair and those steel grey eyes were his undoing. Geoff pulled him into an embrace and thumped him on the back. Kiter was careful hugging him back as Geoff hadn't fully healed from when he was kidnapped and tortured in April. He still had a couple cracked ribs not fully healed yet. But it was good to see him without bruises on his face.

"It's good to see you." Geoff pulled back and held his shoulder smiling his usual friendly grin.

"You too," Kiter agreed. "Am I the last one here?"

"Middle," he answered. "Wilder, Robert, Jenners, and Ira are here still waiting on Godwin, Lee, Raj, Vidar, and Jack. I felt badly when Humail told me he couldn't make it. Said he might try to swing by but with it being after sundown, I doubt it. He came by earlier to drop off some Halal meat and bread for us that his wife made."

"Sounds amazing," Kiter replied. "Haven't had that in a while."

"Same. Better hurry though, the lads are munching on it as we speak."

"How are you feeling?" He asked as they turned toward the library.

"Better, Peter's been taking good care of me," his grin was enough to make Kiter chuckle. As much as he cared for Geoff, loved him even, the idea of he and Peter together made him happy unlike the idea of Rhys with anyone else. That told him volumes that he wasn't ready to dissect yet.

"Your man better be taking good care of you or he'll have to answer to me."

They stepped into the library. "That would only be a threat if I felt threatened," Peter's American accented voice came from nearby. He sauntered over to Geoff and wrapped his arm around his lower back, extending his hand to Kiter. It was a show of possession and Kiter had to laugh when he caught Geoff's eye roll. The men loved each other, it was obvious. And it was clear Peter still thought of Kiter as a potential threat, even if there was no reason for it. He would never get back with Geoff. They were friends but they were completely different men than they had been eighteen years ago.

"Good to see you, Carlisle," Kiter said taking his hand. "Looks like you've been taking care of your man."

"All the time," Peter answered gazing at Geoff with so much love it almost hurt to witness. Then, he took a breath and looked back at Kiter. "Get you a drink?"

"G&T?" Kiter asked.

"Comin' up."

Peter kissed Geoff's temple and walked back into the library bar. Kiter and Geoff stayed standing together. "He really still thinks I have even a possibility with you?"

Geoff chuckled. "No, he knows who I love, he just..." he sighed dreamily. "He's just Peter."

Kiter shook his head. "Well, if he keeps that dreamy look on your face, I'll forgive him."

"What? What dreamy look? I'm Special Forces, I don't get dreamy looks," Geoff teased.

"Oh... you're *special* all right," Kiter teased. A few of his former team members walked over to greet him.

Geoff gave him the two-finger salute as he winked and walked over to Peter mixing a cocktail. Geoff slipped his hand onto the small of Peter's back and Peter leaned into him kissing him briefly. Kiter chuckled when he saw Geoff's hand slide lower cupping Peter's ass and giving it a squeeze. Peter laughed and shook his head. He turned back to Kiter and walked over handing him his drink. He struck up conversation with Ira, Peter, and Geoff as the rest of Team Alice, the best covert retrieval team and Geoff's SRR team arrived. As commanding officer, Kiter usually took a step back from relating to the men he commanded and never joined them at parties, but since none of them were active duty any longer, it was good to be able to talk to them as men and not soldiers.

Once everyone arrived and had a cocktail, Faust came in to tell them dinner was served in the dining room. It still surprised Kiter that Geoff, the seventh Marquess of Garvey and heir to the Dukedom of Torrington would not try to lord his title over everyone. Geoff was one of the most down to earth people he knew. And he was beyond happy he had found his forever with Peter Carlisle.

"So Colonel," Vidar asked. The man was dirty blonde and taller than Leo at nearly six foot five inches, an Englishman with a Swedish mother and a Norwegian footballer father. "What are you working on now? I know you retired from active duty but are you doing anything interesting?"

Kiter swallowed the wine he had in his mouth and nodded. "I am actually. I have an interesting new position. But unfortunately, I can't say much about it."

"Ah, a top-secret gig, huh?" He teased.

"Something like that," he answered. "What about you? Have you thought of what you're going to do now you've retired?"

"Dad is wanting me to join him back in Norway for a time. He thinks it'll make me want to stay and embrace that side of my heritage. I will never want to stay with him." The animosity in his voice told Kiter volumes. Oskar Jørgensen was notorious for his anger on... and off... the pitch.

"What is he doing now?"

"He's retired, living off his money. Has a nice place. I've seen pictures. But there is no way I'd live there... too quiet," Vidar shook his head and a swallow of his wine. "But I need to be doing something. I mean I'm only thirty-six. I retired early and didn't reup this year but I'm thinking that was a mistake."

"You were weapons and bomb disposal, right?" Kiter asked.

He nodded. "Mainly K9 wrangler."

"How is Shiela, Vi? I miss that old thing," Raj asked from the other side of Vidar.

"She's getting old and fat now she has nothing to do," Vidar answered.

Kiter guessed Shiela was their bomb sniffer dog and was proven right when Raj, sitting on Kiter's right leaned over and whispered, "she's our shepherd. He's not talking about his woman."

Kiter chuckled. "Don't know any woman who would appreciate being called old and fat, so I assumed."

Raj laughed. "You could say, if it were his woman, Vidar would be... in the doghouse!" He laughed even harder, and Kiter chuckled along with him. Movement caught his attention and he turned to see Peter leaning toward Geoff, holding his hand. Geoff's face was filled with pain and Kiter immediately wanted to jump up and help.

"Everything all right?" Kiter asked. Everyone's eyes turned to Geoff and Peter.

Peter nodded. "He gets spasms sometimes. It'll pass."

Raj wiped his mouth and hurried to him. As medic of the group, Raj was the best one for the job but it didn't stop Kiter's blood pressure from spiking as he waited for Geoff's face to relax. When it finally did, he looked around the table sheepishly.

"Sorry, lads," Geoff said. "Just sometimes happens."

"You've been through hell, Commander," Wilder, Geoff's second in command and the oldest one at the table said. "We're just glad you're all right."

"Fine now," Geoff answered and covered Peter's hand with his, giving him a soft smile. "I'm good, baby." Peter licked his lips and nodded. "Let's have a toast since all the attention is on us already." The men at the table chuckled. Geoff stood slowly and raised his wine glass. "To Team Alice. The best covert recovery team and best friends a man can have. Without all of you, I wouldn't be here right now,"

"Same." Peter chimed in.

"Thank you all for being here. Peter and I could not be happier to share this evening with you. It is the ten-year anniversary of when we officially met in the hospital, and it's been a wonderful evening. To Team Alice!"

"Alice!" The men shouted, then drank.

Wilder stood after Geoff sat down. "I think it's safe to say, I speak for everyone here when I say, Geoff, you are loved and admired as an amazing commander, soldier, man, and friend. We are so happy you have found the love you so deeply deserve with Peter, and we are looking forward to getting to know him more now that you two aren't going to pull the whole on again off again thing." Geoff and Peter chuckled and gave each other a loving look as they held hands. "We are glad you're both whole and healthy and we look forward to celebrating you two in the future. To Geoff and Peter!"

The men repeated the toast and drank.

"Thank you," Geoff said to Wilder, then, before conversation started again, he locked eyes with Kiter and grinned. "So, Kiter, did you find a date to the party?" Every eye turned to him, and Kiter shook his head.

"Thanks for that," Kiter grunted.

Geoff beamed and took a drink. "Anytime."

"What party?" Dae-Hyun Lee, the sniper's eyes and ears, asked.

"A party where he's supposed to turn up with a date, a *male* date, and show PDA, which we all know he *loves* to do in order to make all those homophobic assholes in Parliament squirm," Geoff said.

"Please tell me the duke will be at this party," Geoff begged asking after his father, though Kiter had noticed he hadn't called the duke *father.*

There was a collective *ooh* and then Kiter spoke. "I believe he will be. My new boss is wanting me to do this because…" he wasn't sure how much he could reveal. "We are christening my new team and it's made up of… individuals who hold more to Geoff's, Peter's, and my persuasion. He says certain members of Parliament are uncomfortable with the idea and he wants me to be the peacock so to speak to mess with them."

"Any takers, lads? Now's your chance to stick it to the man," Geoff said. "And let's face it, there's got to be one of you who's bicurious." Kiter noticed Gareth Godwin and Dae-Hyun

Lee glance at each other and smirk.

"Geoff," Peter whispered then chuckled.

"I agree, Peter," Kiter said. "Let's not do this."

"If you really want to make them squirm," Godwin began, his Welsh accent clear as day. "Lee and I'll show up and pretend to be a throuple."

"Yeah," Lee grinned and turned his handsome Korean face toward him. "We'll do it. We'd be damn good too."

"It's about time you boys came out," Geoff stated. "You've only been married ten years and we only heard you hooking up nearly every night in the barracks."

Godwin's cheeks went pink as Lee laughed. "So sue me, I've got a bit of an exhibitionist kink in me. I like sex in public."

"Maybe not the time to admit that, babe," Godwin said.

"We already knew it," Raj replied.

"How 'bout it, Kiter? I've heard Welshmen like to do it when singing and Korean men have great stamina. Have you had a threesome?" Geoff asked.

"Geoffrey," Peter grunted.

Godwin turned bright pink and Lee threw his head back and laughed. "I do love making him sing," Lee winked and took Godwin's hand.

"And you do have great stamina," Godwin leaned over and kissed his partner.

The team cheered and applauded. Then, "Kiter? What do you think?" Geoff called again.

"I don't think a throuple is needed," Kiter said.

"Awe, no fair," Godwin whined.

"I'll do it," Vidar offered.

Kiter turned to look at him. "What?"

"I'll do it," Vidar said again.

"I'd be game, too," Raj replied. "Hell, a chance to go to a party, eat, *and* stick it to *the man*? I'm all in."

"Ehum…" Kiter muttered looking between the two men sitting next to him.

"There you go, Somm, Vidar or Raj? The Norseman or The Indian. Personally I'd go with the one who published the *Kama Sutra*."

Peter must have given up scolding his boyfriend because he just laughed.

Kiter looked at the two men beside him. Then, without speaking, he lifted his hand and cupped Raj's cheek. The man flinched back. Kiter raised his eyebrows and Raj deflated.

"Sorry. Just… no." Raj said.

"Understandable." Kiter then looked over at Vidar. He looked a little too much like Leo but he could use that to his advantage. Leaning forward, Kiter motioned for him to come toward him with one finger. Vidar moved and Kiter used the same finger to gently stroke his cheek. "It would be for one evening. But you would have to pretend like we've been together for a couple months."

"I've never been with a man but…" Vidar started.

"But?"

Vidar looked sheepish and a blush colored his face. "You've always been curious," Kiter said. Vidar nodded. "Interesting," Kiter answered. "I can work with that." He leaned forward. He felt Vidar's hot breath on his lips and saw Vidar close his eyes. After a beat, never quite closing the gap between them, Kiter pulled away breaking the moment and reached for his wine. Vidar nearly tumbled forward and opened his eyes.

Kiter grinned. "You'll do."

"Damn... that was hot," Geoff said. Peter, Godwin, and Lee all nodded.

Gareth stood quickly, "bathroom?" he questioned, and Dae-Hyun stood. They both hurried off, the sound of the team laughing followed them down the hall.

Vidar reached for his water glass and guzzled the icy drink. Faust was there in a moment with a refill.

"I'll pick you up Saturday night," Kiter said.

Chapter Eight

Picking up Vidar for the Saturday evening party was easy. The man knew how to dress and looked sharp even if he had played with his suit coat a dozen times out of nerves. Kiter glanced over to see him checking his tie again.

"You look good, Vidar," Kiter said. "Don't be so worried."

"I just don't want to mess this up for you," he said.

"I appreciate that. But you won't. And I suppose, there are somethings I need to tell you. A partner would know about my job and honestly... I was thinking about presenting you with an offer."

"An offer?" Kiter felt Vidar turn in his seat to look at him.

"The only reason I hesitate is because of the foundation of this team. We are The Charing Cross Boys. Now whatever I say to you from here on out, if you reveal to anyone other than the people we're talking to tonight, could get someone killed.

Myself included."

"I would never say anything. I'll put it in writing if you need me to. I understand secrecy. I was in SRR."

"Very true, I apologize. I forgot for a moment." Kiter pulled off the road and parked the car. He turned to the other man. "The Charing Cross Boys is named after the station of course. The reason behind it being the six platforms all going to different parts of the world really, now, the Chunnel is completed. Six men, all with special elite skills. We have a thief, a spy, a Royal Marine, and a Paratrooper. We are still recruiting. But the one thing about this team is, it is Parliament's answer to Diversity and Inclusion. Meaning, all members of this team identify as part of the LGBTQ community. Of which you're not. At least, not that I'm aware of."

Vidar shook his head. "I mean... I've always wondered. But I've never... What, um, what sort of ops do you boys do?"

"Well, since this is still very new, we haven't gone on any yet. But these would be considered dangerous, unsanctioned missions. We go where MI6 needs us to go but cannot sanction. We would have room for you, if you would be interested."

"I would have to come out or whatever."

"On paper, yes," Kiter answered.

Vidar paused and then took a deep breath. "My parents... My dad is deeply... homophobic. He had a gay member of his football team, and he always talked badly about him. And... there's some history between he and I. I don't know if I could..."

"I understand. I'm not asking for an answer now. You would have as much time as you would need and if the answer is *no* then that is fine. I appreciate you coming with me tonight."

"Could we... get the first kiss awkwardness out of the

way?" Vidar asked. "I'm worried if you try to kiss me I might freeze."

"Do you want me to kiss you?" Kiter asked. "We don't have to."

Vidar licked his lips. "Yeah. I'm curious"

"All right." Slowly leaning over across the console, Kiter gently cupped the back of Vidar's neck and waited. He would have Vidar come to him. He wouldn't push it. But then he felt Vidar's soft lips on his and he eased into the kiss. As first kisses go, it wasn't the most awkward Kiter had ever experienced, but it was clear Vidar was fighting something inside him. Possibly his father's deeply rooted dislike of gay people. Still, he kissed him gently and it wasn't unpleasant by any means. But he wasn't Rhys. No matter how much he could pass for him in a darkened alley with the height and built, he wasn't his man. And it felt too much like cheating to let it continue. Kiter pulled back and looked into Vidar's eyes, "How was that?"

"Are you fishing for compliments?" Vidar asked.

"If you can joke about it, then it couldn't have been too bad."

"No, actually. It was... kind of nice."

"Good. Let's get going then, we're going to be late."

Kiter and Vidar leaned back in their seats as Kiter put the car into gear.

They arrived at the venue and were greeted by Lester. "Kiter! I worried you might not come."

"My apologies, sir, but when you have a gorgeous man on your arm you sometimes lose track of time," Kiter held Vidar close. Though he was a good five inches shorter than the Norseman, he still felt protective of him.

"Indeed, well hello. You must be Vidar, am I saying that correctly?" Lester offered his hand.

"Yes, sir," Vidar answered. "And you must be Commander Lester. Sommerset has told me so much about you."

Kiter held in his chuckle. He had told him literally nothing other than the man's name on the way in when they spotted him walking toward them.

"Trust me, I'm sure he has. I don't make his life easy."

"No, definitely not, but he is doing something he loves and hey, I'm not complaining when he takes his frustrations out on me in bed. So please, keep it up." Vidar wiggled his eyebrows suggestively.

Kiter nearly choked on his own spit. Vidar was better at this than he knew.

"Oh perfect!" Lester clapped his hands. "He's bloody perfect, Kiter. Wherever you found him."

"Vidar and I have known each other for nearly ten years, Commander," Kiter explained.

"Well, good. Let me introduce you to a few people. Can I get you a drink?" Lester asked.

"I'll have a glass of dry red please," Vidar said. "Babe?" he asked turning to Kiter.

"I'll do a whiskey," Kiter said.

"Don't go away. I'll be right back." With that, Lester walked away toward the bar.

"You..." Kiter breathed a chuckle. "Well, remind me to send a gift basket to Geoff and Peter for their suggestion."

Vidar chuckled. "I just thought what I'd want to hear and said it. Not sure if I'm doing anything right."

"There's no wrong way. Just don't maybe mention a

girlfriend."

"Definitely won't do that."

"Kiter," they heard and turned to the owner of the voice. "Good to see you. And who is this?"

The evening progressed much the same as Kiter and his team was celebrated and Vidar was introduced as his partner. Vidar played his part to perfection even going so far as defending Kiter against Geoff's homophobic arsehole father, The Duke of Torrington.

As they both headed to the bar to get another drink, Kiter leaned closer to Vidar. "Thank you," he said.

Vidar turned to look at him. "For what?"

"For everything tonight. It means a lot to me the things you said. I appreciate you defending me against the duke."

"That arsehole," Vidar replied. "He needed to be put in his place. I can't imagine someone as amazing as Geoff being raised by that tosser."

"He wasn't," Kiter explained. "Geoff was sent to boarding school at six years old. He and the duke hate each other."

"Makes sense. Sorry for nearly mauling you, though, I needed to make him shut up."

"I'm not complaining. I don't mind hard kisses," Kiter teased.

Vidar chuckled. "Thank you. It's been entertaining being here tonight."

"It has. Thank you."

"Maybe we can hang out again? You know, not as a couple or anything, but get a beer sometime."

"You're straight, I would never want to give the impression nor make you uncomfortable," Kiter said.

Vidar stared at him for a long moment. "Not that straight," he admitted. "But I've... never said that out loud."

Kiter covered his hand with his own. "You're safe here with me. Thank you for trusting me."

Tears gathered in Vidar's eyes, and he let out a harsh breath. "Fuck. I've never said that before. It feels... so good to finally admit."

"I understand." Kiter smiled softly. "Hey, it's okay."

Vidar took a deep breath and nodded, then let out the breath through puffed cheeks. Movement caught his eye and Kiter watched a look come over his face. His slack jawed stunned expression was interesting. Vidar clearly saw something or someone who interested him.

"Hey handsome, what's your pleasure?" A very familiar voice said from behind the counter.

Vidar's face went red as a fierce blush colored his cheeks. "Uh, ehm, I, um..."

"Cutie at a loss for words," the bartender winked, and Kiter shook his head, leaning over the counter.

"What are you doing here, Boyd?" Kiter hissed.

"Had to come and see what the fuss was about, Daddy," Boyd teased. "Though I have to say you picked a good one. Damn. Seeing you both out there working the room, it's hot."

Vidar made a squeaking sound, which for a man of his stature was quite comical.

"So what's your name, handsome?" Boyd turned to Vidar.

Vidar stumbled over his words as he finally said, "Víðarr," pronouncing it in his native language.

Boyd glanced over at Kiter, an eyebrow raised. "Vidar

Jørgensen, meet Agent Boyd Falstaff. Boyd is currently on my team. Boyd, this is Vidar, he was in my platoon in the military. Be nice."

"I'm always nice, Daddy," Boyd answered. "It just depends on how nice you want me to be. And in your case, Thor, I'd climb you like a tree and never let go."

Vidar nearly choked on his own spit, at least that was what it sounded like as he coughed and sputtered. Boyd's lips turned up in a sassy smirk.

"He's hot, Daddy," Boyd looked over at Kiter. "Let me get those drinks."

Kiter watched Vidar watching Boyd leave. His eyes were firmly glued to Boyd's backside. And as he watched Vidar watch Boyd mix the drinks, almost like he had put some sort of spell on him, Kiter wondered when Vidar would accept his offer to join the CCB.

Chapter Nine

It was one week later when a knock came on Rhys' front door. Coming out of his martial arts form, he sheathed his *katana* and walked to the door. Wiping the sweat from his forehead, he opened the door and came face to face with Kiter. The man's eyes immediately fell to Rhys' bare chest.

"Uh," he so eloquently said. "Good morning."

Refusing to be self-conscious, Leo stood in the doorway, his Samurai Sword still sheathed and clutched in his hand. "What do you want?"

Kiter licked his lips and blinked a few times then finally looked up at him. "Please don't let me interrupt."

Scoffing, Rhys turned around, leaving the door open and preceded to remount the Samurai sword back on the wall and taking a step back, he lowered his head toward it giving the respect he had learned from his time in Japan. He heard and felt

Kiter move from the hallway into his space but kept his distance from him. "What do you want?" Leo asked again.

"I realize not telling you about my involvement and springing Boyd on you was not the best idea," Kiter began.

"Gee, ya think?" He pulled on his t-shirt over his *hakama* pants.

"But I honestly didn't know how to tell you about my involvement. Would you believe me if I said I chose you for your skills?"

He laughed humorlessly. "Yeah, right. A forty-two-year-old nearly crippled veteran? I would have believed you if you had told me that ten years ago."

"You are not nearly crippled," Kiter defended.

"But honestly, this whole thing is fucked up," Leo said grabbing a bottled water from his fridge. "My boss told me you haven't sent the paperwork over yet. Can I ask what the hell is taking you so long?" He guzzled half the bottle in one go and ignored how Kiter watched his throat work.

"I was hoping we could talk."

Leo stared at him for the longest time but said nothing. Did he hate Kiter's involvement in the job he truly wanted? Yes. Did he hate the idea of working beside two men who broke his trust beyond reconciliation? Yes. Did he want the job and knew he was the best choice for it? Hell yes. But that didn't matter.

"Thanks for stopping by, Colonel. But there's nothing for you here."

"Dammit, Leo why do you have to be so damn stubborn?" Kiter demanded.

"Character trait," he shrugged.

"Tell you what," Kiter began and stuffed his hands in the

pockets of his jeans. "Look me in the eye and tell me you don't want this job. To get in on the ground level of this team. To have exciting missions with an element of fear to season it. To defend the nation from all threats. Tell me that and I'll sign the paperwork today."

Rhys paused, drank more from his water bottle, then shook his head. "Not the way it is currently."

"What would make you happy? My resignation? Boyd's? What is it you want?"

"I don't want this," he motioned between them. "I don't want you ruling my life, my career. I want the job, yes, dammit I do. But not with the lies and secrets that begat it."

"There are no more lies. No more secrets," Kiter promised.

"With you? There always are. So, forgive me if I don't trust your word."

Kiter stared at him for a long moment. "So that's it then," he finally said. "That's what you want. Me out of your life."

"I've wanted that for nearly twenty years," Leo replied.

Kiter swallowed hard and blinked his eyes. Then, with a breath, he nodded. "I'll – uhm – have your transfer papers signed and couriered over to your old department." He paused. "For what it's worth, I'm sorry. For everything, Rhys. This is not what I wanted and I'm sorry it's what happened. I thought... I thought we were on the mend. I didn't think you would hate me so much..." He took a few steps over to Leo and tentatively placed his hand on Leo's arm. Leo tried not to flinch. "Be well. Be happy. That's all I've ever wanted." Kiter squeezed his arm and walked backwards a couple steps. Leo had a distinct impression Kiter was memorizing his face. Eventually, Kiter turned his back, his shoulders rose and fell on a breath. Then, without turning back, he said, "I love you, Rhys. I always have and I always will. Please, no matter what happens, do not think of me with anger. Please remember the good times, as I will."

With that, Sommerset Kiter opened the door and walked out of Rhys Campbell's life forever. Leo didn't expect the lump to form in his throat so quickly nor the tears to gather in his eyes. It was over. He'd never see him again. Leo wasn't sure why that thought made him sob.

Chapter Ten

The first mission was supposed to be easy. Kiter looked up as the boardroom door opened and his team walked in. Darius and Hesler, the new recruits, had agreed to join the team together. The two men held hands as they walked in and Kiter saw the engagement rings on their fingers and smiled. Their little vacation had wound up being an engagement party.

Callum walked in next with Boyd. Taking their seats, Kiter read the room. Hesler being a Royal Marine and Darius as a Paratrooper kept their expressions neutral. A trait Kiter had come to expect from former active-duty military. Callum, as leader, sat apart from the other three and commanded the respect that was due to him easily. He was a natural born leader and having been to hell and back a couple times helped keep his expression calm. Boyd on the other hand, looked... nervous. He hid it well beneath a playful façade, but Kiter could see deep down he was scared. And he should be. It was his first mission. His first trip outside of the UK and he didn't know what to expect. He was trained in shooting by Callum but wasn't a good shot, no matter how steady his hands were. He was lean but he had muscles on him, and Kiter had supervised his hand-to-hand combat training over the last month and a half. The team had eight weeks together and though they were a good set of boys, they weren't a team yet. That was where Kiter knew he had to step in, but his mind was distracted with thoughts of Rhys. He hadn't heard from him, and he wouldn't reach out, couldn't. Leo had told him he wanted him out of his life. He would respect that. But it didn't help when he was trying to prep for a mission. That would make or break the team. Let alone one he would have men's lives at stake.

But the mission was an easy one.

"Good morning," he began once they all sat. He received the expected answer and continued. "Our first op." He clicked on the computer and the face of the expat filled the screen. The door opened and Commander Lester entered. He smiled quickly and nodded indicating Kiter to continue and took a seat near the door. "Hasan Petra, British national, born in London, graduated top of his class at the University of London. Began working with MI6 in Counter Terrorism after the September 11th Attacks. Repeatedly on record of having sympathies to the attackers and a citation on file for proactively engaging in antigovernment antiBritish rallies. Was blacklisted after evidence was discovered he was behind the London Bridge bombing that was stopped by one of our own. It was thought he had died in an altercation with the agent and fell into the Thames, until six days later his car was discovered at a train station terminal, and a file he had been working on at work was missing. This file contains pertinent information regarding British nuclear warheads. The design, and more importantly how to disable the launch sequence and initiate self destruct. Since this discovery, the engineers have been working on changing the protocol, but it seems that is not something that is easily done. There have been rumblings from our agents in the field in Moscow and Kandahar of a new player in the business. These rumblings were confirmed by our agent inside the Kremlin when he caught wind of a brokered deal with a British agent and a Russian FSB. That deal was the plans and protocols for the bombs. The agent had visual, and the documents are genuine. The agent could not get his hands on them without arousing suspicion, and it is thought Petra has copies. Another agent has contacted us with information of Petra reaching out to the Kabul offering the same documents.

"Our mission is to stop Petra from meeting them in Maldives," he switched the picture to a drone shot of a mansion overlooking the beach. "This is Petra's fortress. The funds he received from Russia and other countries for his knowledge has given him the means to protect himself. Last count, there were two dozen guards, a half dozen SAMs, and a sheer rock face on the North and South of the building. We have confirmation Petra will be at this location in two days time giving a house party. The proposed plan is an amphibious attack from a mile out to this cave. The cave is not as heavily guarded and provides indirect access to the house. There are cameras, as that is where Petra keeps his yacht. We need to disable the boat so there is no escape and enter as quietly as possible through the door to the kitchen where you can blend in with the waitstaff. Then we split into two teams. Callum and Hesler, you two go up to find Petra while Darius and Boyd you find the safe with the papers. The safe is located here with complex security measures." He switched to another picture using infrared. The large black box in the middle of the screen showed the safe was on the northeast side of the building.

"Do you know the style?" Boyd asked.

"Unclear exactly, but I would expect biometrics."

"Which means computer, which means hacking. Got it," Boyd nodded.

"What sort of timeframe we looking at?" Hesler asked.

"In and out in thirty," Kiter explained. "Keep low, stay quick. Once Petra is in your custody, you will move to the east side of the building out to the beach where they keep the dinghies, and I will meet you. We drive through to Australian waters where we drop him in the dinghy and call the Australian Coast Guard. Then we head to International Waters and are picked up by a British sub here." He showed the X on the map.

"If there's a beach with dinghies, why don't we just attack from there instead?" Callum questioned.

"Because that area is guarded by the surface-to-air missiles and drones."

"So how do we get out?" Darius asked.

"They are programmed to attack incoming not outgoing forces." The team was quiet for a long moment. Then Kiter continued. "Any other questions?" When no one spoke, Lester stood. "Commander, would you like to say a few words?" Kiter asked.

The team turned to look and made to stand but Lester waved them off as he walked to the front of the group. "These are the types of missions we need this team for. You each have a special set of skills and together you will succeed. This quick smash and grab will prove your team is ready to take on more detailed missions and I for one cannot wait to see how it all goes. Now, be sure to check in and let's get started."

Kiter turned to his team. "With that, get home, get some sleep, we're wheels up at 0900. We'll land at an airfield in Columbo, stay the night then drive the boat to the location in the early afternoon. Join the party by 1700. Dismissed."

The four men stood and gathered their things. Once alone with Lester, Kiter turned to his commander. "Why do I have a bad feeling about this?"

Lester waved him off. "They'll be fine, Kiter. You have to know that. It's an easy mission. In and out. Nothing major. Keep me updated."

With that, he left the room leaving Kiter alone. Taking a deep breath, he closed his eyes and hoped.

The flight and boat ride had gone according to plan and as Kiter stood looking at Callum, Boyd, Hesler, and Darius the next afternoon dressed in their diving suits, he pushed down the concern he had and checked their air tanks.

"All set?" He asked. They nodded. "All right, you boys know your assignments, take care of each other out there. Make it back here safely. Don't wander off, don't dawdle and don't die. You check in when I ask, and you keep me updated if there's anything we didn't expect. Listen to Fraxinus and get back here. Understood?"

"Understood," they all said.

"Good, I'll see you all back here in thirty minutes."

Kiter watched as all four men sat on the edge of the boat and followed Callum's lead pushing backwards off the side into the water to swim the mile to the shore. Taking his binoculars, Kiter watched the bubbles until he saw Hesler and Darius surface under the arch of the cave housing the yacht.

"Charing Cross, come in, status?" Kiter asked as he saw the two men stow their oxygen tanks behind the rocks.

"This is Copperhead," Hesler spoke low. "Fraxinus and Autolycus are disabling the rudder and engine of the yacht."

"Affirmative, hold your position, Copperhead. See if you can spot any of the cameras."

"Cameras made, attempting disable now," Darius said. Just as he spoke Callum and Boyd surfaced and walked up the rocky beach. Quickly removing their gear and stripping out of their wet suits to their waitstaff tuxes underneath, Callum spoke.

"Scorpio, this is Fraxinus," Callum spoke. "We are cleared. Getting in position."

"Confirmed, Fraxinus, mission is a go. Be careful," Kiter said. With a breath, Kiter watched Callum lead the team up the stairs of the cave. When they were out of sight, Kiter moved from the bow of the ship to the pilot house and watched the body cams seeing his boys climb the stairs.

After a beat, Kiter heard Darius. "Scorpio, come in."

"Go for Scorpio," Kiter said.

"You said this is a party?"

"Affirmative," Kiter answered. "Why?"

"There's no music. There are no voices," Darius explained.

Kiter paused debating. "Keep to the plan. Find Petra and get back here."

"Understood," that was Callum. "Scorpio, we've reached the top," Callum continued after a long pause. "Copperhead is right. There's no music, no voices, it's dead up here."

"Keep sharp. Intel hot," Kiter stated.

He waited a little longer watching the cams. They reached the kitchen door but what should have been open was locked.

"Autolycus," Callum said to Boyd.

"On it," Boyd picked the lock in under two seconds. For a thief, Boyd picked the best codename for himself.

They were in, but everything was dark.

"Scorpio, something isn't right. There are no lights on, nothing," Callum said.

"Do a sweep, see if you can find Petra. If you can't, get out of there."

"Understood," he replied. "CCB, Platform 5."

It was their code for be alert and get weapons drawn. They set their packs down and got their weapons out along with their Kevlar vests and night vision. Kiter watched as they switched to night vision and cased the room. Originally, they were only to have a knife on them for defense, but Kiter fought Lester on it, and they were given M4s just in case. He was glad at that moment. Even Boyd, though not the best shot, still had a gun. They cased the kitchen finding nothing. Moving into the main part of the house, they stopped cold.

"Scorpio, we've got a problem."

"What do you see?" Kiter tried to squint but it was dark and night vision on the cameras was fuzzy.

"Bodies, lots of them," Callum said and swept the main living room. The blood was easily seen. About thirty bodies were strewn around the room. Men and women in party dress, some of the bodyguards, and a few waitstaff.

"Oh god," Boyd groaned and promptly vomited into a potted plant.

Darius moved toward him. "Breathe through your mouth, Autolycus. You'll be okay."

"Copperhead, get him out of here," Callum ordered. Boyd's and Darius' cameras showed they were retreating back the way they came.

"Fraxinus, talk to me. Can you see how they were killed?" Kiter questioned.

"GSWs to the head, execution style. We dealing with cartels, Scorpio?"

"No intel. Can you identify our mark?"

"Standby," Callum said. He and Hesler gingerly stepped around the bodies looking for Petra. Kiter looked over to see Darius and Boyd still making their way slowly but steadily to the beach with the dinghies.

"Scorpio, confirmed. Petra is here," Hesler said.

"Dead?" Kiter looked over at Callum's camera feed.

"Affirmative," Callum stated.

Hesler cursed. "Scorpio, his eyes and ring finger are missing."

"Shite," Kiter cursed. "Rentai Cartel. That's their calling card. Get a picture and get the hell out of there."

"Acknowledged," Just as Callum got the photograph of their mark, Kiter heard the popping sound of gunfire.

"Autolycus, Copperhead come in," Kiter ordered looking

at their cameras.

"Scorpio! We're entrenched over here. Taking heavy fire. Twenty to thirty tangos. Shit, they were waiting for us!" Darius shouted as he and Boyd took cover behind a boulder.

"Retreat back to the cave," Kiter ordered.

"Negative, we're surrounded," Darius replied.

"Copperhead, we're on our way," Hesler called over the comms as he and Callum raced out of the house and down toward the beach.

"The SAMs and drones aren't taking these guys out!" Darius shouted over the gunfire.

"It must have been sabotaged. Fraxinus, Ryker, how far are you?" Kiter demanded.

"We're here," Callum said as he took out two guys in front of him.

"Thank god," Boyd grunted and got up to run to the team.

"Boyd, no!" Darius shouted and lunged for him. Just as he tackled him to the sand, there was a sound, one Kiter knew all too well, a bullet shooting through Kevlar and hitting a body.

"Copperhead!" Kiter shouted.

"Darius!" Hesler screamed at his fiancé.

"He's hit!" Boyd shouted from beneath Darius' body. He wiggled out and dragged him to safety.

Kiter put the boat into gear and zoomed through the water. The popping sound of gunfire continued, and Kiter watched as he got to the cave.

"I'm in the cave, can you get here?"

There was no answer as the firefight continued. He watched the camera seeing Hesler reach Darius. He was still alive and awake, but blood was seeping out of his mouth.

"Stay with me, baby," Hesler ordered as he pulled off his fiancé's vest.

Someone had tipped off the cartel. Someone wanted his team dead, and Kiter swore then, he would find the bastard.

"We're outnumbered here!" Callum yelled.

"Charing Cross retreat! Retreat to the cave!" Kiter shouted.

Callum grabbed the back of Boyd's vest and yanked him back as they both fired their weapons.

"Ryker, give me a status on Copperhead," Kiter ordered.

"Not good," was all Ryker said. "Baby, come on. Stay with me."

Kiter could see the blood seeping out of Darius' mouth and through Hesler's body cam he watched as Darius weakly reached up and cupped Hesler's jaw. The look on Darius' face was gentle but resigned.

"I love you," he said softly.

Hesler covered Darius' hand with his. "I love you too." After a pause, Darius' eyes glazed, and the wet breathing stopped. "Dare. Dare, no please." Hesler begged. "Come on, baby, don't. No, don't leave me."

Kiter closed his eyes. He hadn't lost a man on active duty for nearly fifteen years. He was their leader. He felt Hesler's pain as if it was his own.

"Ryker, fall back!" Callum shouted over the gun fire. "Fall back! Autolycus, Ryker! Now, dammit."

"What about Darius?" Boyd cried.

"There's nothing we can do now. Fall back. Go! Get to the cave. Scorpio, we're on our way."

"Affirmative," Kiter choked out.

"Ryker! Ryker, fall back, dammit! I said fall back! That's an order!" Callum shouted. Kiter glanced down at Darius' cam seeing Hesler still over his body. The look on Hesler's face gave him pause.

"Ryker, that's an order. Fall back!" Kiter demanded.

"No," Hesler replied then looking up at Callum he shouted. "There's no world for me without him in it. Go! Get out of here! I'll cover you."

"Ryker!" Callum shouted, but it was too late. Ryker had leaned down and kissed Darius, then picked up both his and Darius' M4 and turned to the enemy. With a shout, he began firing.

Kiter swallowed hard but gave another order, this time to Callum. "Fraxinus, fall back. Get to the caves."

"What about Darius and Hesler?" Boyd protested as Callum pushed him further down the steps to the cave.

"There's nothing we can do for them now, move!" They raced to the water and jumped in. Reaching the boat, they pulled themselves up and as soon as they were clear, Kiter put the boat in gear and raced off. Boyd ran up the deck to the pilot house, but Kiter locked the door. He knew Boyd wanted to watch the feed, but he couldn't let him.

"Let me in!" Boyd banged on the door. Kiter wouldn't let the boy have the images in his mind that Kiter was seeing. At last count, Hesler had taken five bullets but still the former Royal Marine was standing and firing. He had reloaded both M4s and had killed about fifteen of the thirty men. But he was down to the last five rounds.

"Let me in!" Boyd shouted again. Then, the sound of the

lock sliding back alerted Kiter that the master thief had picked the lock.

"Fraxinus, remove him," Kiter shouted when the door opened.

"No!" Boyd screamed as Callum wrapped his arms around him from behind in a bear hug and forcibly removed him from the pilot house. "I want to see! I need to know! He's dead because of me."

"No, that's not true, Boyd," Callum said as they exited the room. "He protected you. His choice. Come on."

The door slid shut just as another shot rang out on the cams. Hesler was hit. He fell back, landing across Darius' body, his breathing labored. The frame looked down as Hesler looked at his hands, covered in blood.

"Scorpio, I'm sorry," Hesler panted.

"No, no Hes, *I'm* sorry."

"Get these sons of bitches, aye?" Hesler wheezed.

"I will. Godspeed, Marine."

There was no reply and Kiter knew he was gone.

Chapter Eleven

"That's a wrap, gentlemen, good work." Leo slapped his right-hand man, Nigel Sweet on the shoulder as his four-man team all arrived safely back at Police Headquarters and headed down to the locker rooms to shower and change from their SWAT outfits.

"Tell you what, boss, I don't know how you do it," another of his team Gabe Collins said.

"Yeah boss, those guys were brutal. How'd you talk 'em down like that?" Sweet questioned.

"It's a gift," Leo shrugged.

"What language were you speaking? I thought I knew all your secrets. Never heard you talking like that," Sweet continued as they made it to their assigned lockers.

It was a hot day in London and Rhys needed a wonderfully cool shower after sweating his balls off for hours in their riot gear talking a suicidal extremist out of taking half of Stratford with him as he wept claiming the world was evil. Which Rhys didn't disagree with but was fortunate his language skills came into play. The man was merely distraught as his daughter had been assaulted by men in the area. Rhys didn't blame the man. He was sure he would do the same if it had been his family.

"You don't know all my tricks, Sweet," Leo chuckled pulling off his body armor with a sigh of relief.

"Not by a long shot," Collins said and smacked Sweet on the ass with a towel as he stripped to his tighty-whities.

"You wish, handsome," Sweet winked, teasing his best mate.

"Ugh, just kiss already," the fourth man, Stan Bethel groaned, grabbing his toiletries and heading into the showers.

"You'd like that, Bethel!" Sweet called after him. Then, he lowered his voice and muttered. "Homophobic arsehole."

"He just doesn't get it," Collins replied. "Don't let it get to you."

"Easy for you to say. You didn't have to fight for equality for hundreds of years," Sweet replied.

"Neither did you," Collins answered. "Unless you're some five-hundred-year-old vampire I don't know about," he winked. "Which wouldn't be true since I've known you since you were sixteen."

"You never know. I still could be," Sweet grinned back and gave a fake vampiric hiss showing his teeth. "Besides it's the principle of the thing."

"Ah, yes of course. How silly of me. Forgive me, Sweets," Collins said using his nickname for him.

"We have more freedom now than ever before, Nige. Don't forget that," Leo stated. "I for one, just want to be able to live my life how and with whomever I please."

"Speaking of," Collins leaned against the lockers near Leo, a towel wrapped around his waist. "How did that date go?"

"You sure you're straight, Gabe?" Sweet asked, walking past him buck naked heading to the showers. Leo caught Collins glancing at Sweet's ass and rose an eyebrow seeing the light pink tinging Gabe's cheeks.

"Is it a crime to be interested in how my boss' date went?" Collins asked.

"No," Leo answered as they walked to the showers. "But it is weird."

"So you didn't get laid?" Collins asked.

"Inappropriate is the word that comes to mind," Leo replied moving into a stall and pulling off his towel.

"Oh come on, boss," Collins did the same taking the stall between Sweet and Leo. "I'm an old married man. I gotta live vicariously though you."

Leo's heavy sigh echoed against the walls as he turned on the water. "It was... okay."

"Okay?" Sweet and Collins said at the same time. "You didn't fancy him?"

"He was nice. The location was fun. The food was good," Leo listed.

"So... it all fell apart in the bedroom?" Sweet asked.

Bethel made a disgusted sound and turned off the water. Wrapping the towel around his waist, he walked out of the showers back to the locker room.

"We have got to do something about him," Sweet said

softly.

"Yeah, I don't feel like any of us can be ourselves around him," Collins agreed.

"Can't do anything, you know that," Leo answered. "He's the chief's nephew. Just don't let it bother you."

"Yeah, you're right. So... we were talking about the bedroom," Collins prompted.

"We didn't get that far," Leo admitted.

"What?" Sweet asked.

"Why?" Collins questioned.

Leo chuckled. "Because I'm allergic to peanuts and he ordered his burger with peanut butter then asked why I wouldn't kiss him. I told him I like breathing too much. He called me a prude and said he didn't believe I had an allergy and claimed I was making it up. He grabbed me and forced his lips on mine."

"Shit," Collins breathed.

"Bad move to pull on a Samurai," Sweet said.

"I'm not a Samurai. I'm a black belt in Jujitsu and own a Katana but there's a difference. It would be an honor to be a Samurai, but they unfortunately no longer exist like they used to."

"Yes yes, history lesson aside," Sweet interrupted. "What happened?"

"He was on his back with a sprained wrist and knee before I realized my throat was closing up. Got my epipen and only then did he realize I was telling the truth and hovered over me trying to help. He called an ambulance, and it took us both to get checked out. He kept apologizing during the ride. I ignored him. Then, once we were cleared by the doctors, he came up to me and asked for another chance."

"Nope," Sweet shook his head.

"Definitely not. Tell me you didn't, boss," Collins said.

"Do I look like I have a death wish?" Leo countered. "I said no and thanked him for the experience. Said it was memorable, but never again."

"And how did he take it?"

"Surprisingly well."

"Good riddance, then. Have some respect for boundaries, yeah?" Sweet replied. "Was this an app hookup?"

"No, met him at the market, actually. We were both reaching for the spaghetti sauce."

"Good meet cute, but terrible experience. Sorry about that, Boss," Collins said. "Look, I'll talk to Amelie and see if we know anyone single. We'll get you laid."

Leo chuckled while rinsing his hair. "Please don't. I'm good."

"You'll get a muscle cramp in your arm if you don't get some soon," Collins said.

"Gabbie, baby, please TMI, mate. I don't need to know your habits," Sweet winked. "Tell me more," he wiggled his eyebrows.

Leo and Collins chuckled. Finished with their showers, they dried off and got dress. Bending to pull on his trainers, Leo groaned. His back and knee were acting up. "Gonna rain tonight."

"Oh, nah, boss, don't tell me that. We got football tonight," Collins said pulling on his baseball cap.

"Oh, do the boys play tonight?" Sweet asked excitedly.

"Yeah, they do. Hey, you should come. Amelie can't make

it. Something about her book club getting together."

"Don't they usually get together on Mondays?" Leo asked.

"I guess, I don't keep up with the schedule," Collins said. "But you're both welcome."

"I can't," Leo apologized. "Got a hot date with my hand." He winked.

Collins laughed. "What about you, Sweets? The boys would love to see you."

"I'll... ehm... see. I don't know what I have planned tonight. You know me, everything's on my phone," Sweet turned away to put his toiletries back in the locker.

"Okay, mate, well, I'll text you the details. See you lads later," Collins touched the brim of his hat in a wave and left the locker room. Sweet let out a soft sigh and watched him go Leo leaned against the locker next to him.

"You know, pining after him will get you no where. He's married with kids. And straight," Leo said gently.

Sweet looked over and shrugged. "Clichéd right? Gay guy in love with his straight best friend? Who would have thought it... oh that's right, every romcom ever made."

Leo stood straight and placed his hands on Sweet's shoulders. "I just don't want to see you get hurt."

"I know. Thanks, boss. I'm fine. I out with guys. I hookup. It's not like I'm waiting for him."

"Good. But how many of those hookups do you see again?"

"None, that's the point of a hookup."

Leo shook his head gently. "Nigel..."

"Rhys, please don't..." Sweet tried. Leo took a breath and

nodded. Sweet turned to him with a forced fake smile. "What a pair we are, huh?" he closed his locker door and turned to him. "Me pining for my straight best friend. You nursing a heartbreak and pining for your former one."

Taking a step back and grabbing his bag, Leo closed himself off. "I don't know what you're talking about." But the image of Kiter standing in his flat two months ago, and the look on his face when he told him he never wanted to see him again flashed before his eyes. God, it had been over two months, and he hadn't heard anything from him. Fear he could be hurt on any of those dangerous missions, anger that he had lied to him, hurt that he didn't trust him enough to tell him the whole truth, all the emotions floating around him but mainly the fear he might never see Sommerset again. Then, he mentally kicked himself because he never did want to see him again. He meant nothing to him. But Leo knew that was a lie. He always loved him, even when it hurt like hell.

"I need to brief the super," Leo said.

"Think you could do anything about Bethel?" Sweet asked.

There was something in his eyes that gave Leo pause. He took a step toward him. "Has he threatened you?"

"No," Sweet took a quick step back and shook his head too adamantly. "He just... makes me uncomfortable. I can't quite put my finger on it."

"I'll see what I can do."

"Thanks, boss."

"Promise me you won't torture yourself and go to the game tonight."

"I can't do that," Sweet said.

"Nigel, I'm serious."

"I know you are. But I can't promise that. I can promise to pull up my hookup app after I say goodbye, though."

Leo shook his head but knew it was a lost cause. With a quick *okay* and a *see you tomorrow,* Leo left the locker room alone with his thoughts and that was one place Leo never wanted to be.

Chapter Twelve

Kiter walked into his offices to see Marjorie behind her desk. She immediately stood and hurried over to him. He could see her eyes were rimmed red and puffy as if she'd been crying. No surprise. She was in charge of listening and watching the videos of all the missions to analyze what went right and what went wrong. She would have heard and seen Hesler and Darius die, like he did. She said nothing as she wrapped him in a warm embrace. He was grateful for her support but mainly her silence. Lester's boss needed an ass to chew for the deaths of two agents and it happened to be his. Lester had sat in the room, face impassive, but they both knew it could mark the end of the Charing Cross Boys. They needed an easy mission to ease them into the hearts and minds of Parliament, but that mission had been the farthest from easy Kiter had ever faced, and he had stared down the Taliban, ISIS, and al-Qaeda.

But it wasn't just dumb chance that the Rentai Cartel was waiting for them and having killed their mark. Someone, with knowledge of their mission, had tipped them off and Kiter suspected everyone and no one as any good investigator should. The only ones exempt from suspicion were Boyd, Callum, and Marjorie. And to his embarrassment and guilt, he had waited to add her to the list until the moment her red rimmed eyes locked with his and her soft arms wrapped around his waist.

Kiter was half surprised the team wasn't shut down that day but a gentle word from Lester to his boss had cooled that particular desire. Instead, they were all given leave and were told to come back in two weeks with their heads on straight. But a direct punishment for him was that he was in charge of letting Darius' and Hesler's families know their boys, who had just gotten engaged and had their whole lives ahead of them, were dead. Worse of all, since their mission wasn't sanctioned, he had to lie to their faces and not tell them how the brave men who sacrificed their lives for their teammates had died. That was the hardest part of the job.

Marjorie pulled back and stared at him. Her gaze the kind of motherly concern he expected from her, even if she was only ten years older than he was. Her eyes were filling with tears again as she stared at him. *Good,* he thought. *Someone needs to cry for the boys.* Kiter was the leader, he couldn't cry. At least not yet. Not until he was alone. And he didn't want to be alone.

"Boyd and Callum in there?" He asked motioning to the boardroom. She nodded. He stepped out of her hold and squeezed her hands. "Thank you."

"Go easy on the boy. He's taking it hard," she said.

"Yeah, wouldn't surprise me if he quits. If they both don't

quit."

"Don't underestimate Callum's loyalty to you and the program," she replied. "But you need a unifier. Someone who can read them both and keep them together. I would say you but..."

"I know," he admitted. "Deep down they blame me."

"That's not what I meant," she said firmly.

"You'd be right though. It is my fault."

"No," she stressed. "Rentai was waiting for you. That means someone tipped them off."

"Or they were after our mark too, got to him before we did and Darius and Hesler were killed in the crossfire."

"Come on, you and I both know that would be one hell of a coincidence. And we don't believe in coincidences."

Kiter grunted in agreement, then took a step around her. "Let me see if I can salvage my team."

"Be real with them. As real as you are with me. They deserve to see you're hurting too."

With a forced smile, he headed to the board room and opened the door. Two sets of eyes turned to him. One set looked determined, the other apprehensive and it surprised him to see which one was which.

"What did they say?" Callum questioned apprehensively.

"Can we go after the bastards who killed Darius and Hes?" Boyd's look of determination was older than his twenty-one years.

"Boss?" Callum pressed.

"We are still active. They want us to take a couple weeks and then go from there. There's going to be an internal investigation. Answer any and all questions truthfully without thought to who or what they want."

"You're going to let them heap the blame on you? It's not your fault." Callum stepped toward him.

"I'm as good as any scapegoat and I don't want either of you to have to worry about it. Like I said, answer all questions truthfully. Let the pieces fall where they may."

"No, they'll twist our words even if we answer truthfully. I've seen movies like this. I won't let it happen," Boyd said.

"This isn't a damn movie!" Kiter exploded. "You work for me. I tell you to answer all questions truthfully and honestly. And that is an order, dammit."

"I'm not a soldier." Boyd crossed his arms over his chest.

"You are now."

"We were set up! There will be a coverup," Boyd shouted. "This is bullshit."

"Government at it's finest," Callum muttered.

"Look," Kiter paused, closed his eyes and took a deep breath. "I know, believe me, I know how you feel." He opened his eyes and looked at them both individually. "But going rogue isn't going to help the situation, okay?"

"It'd make me feel better," Boyd grumbled. "He died saving my sorry excuse of a life. Because of me both Darius and Hesler are gone."

"That is not true," Kiter stated. "You were caught unawares in a firefight. That was something Darius had experience in, you have no experience as a soldier. He protected you like his oath demanded of him. He did so willingly, and I choose to believe they are looking down on us here now and saying the exact same thing. They wouldn't want us to be angry that's not how they lived. And that's not how they died. I led you.

I got you into this. They are dead because of this mission. My mission. So don't think for one second, I don't feel the weight of their deaths just as much, no more so than you do. Boyd, yes you were there when Darius was shot, but you were unbelievably brave for someone who had never seen battle. And Callum, yes, you were Team Leader out there, but you were following *my* orders. This whole shitshow is on me, lads. *I've* let you down and I've let Darius and Hesler down. So, do not think for one second any of this is on you.

"I'm just as angry as you are. But we are grounded, and an investigation will be conducted where they may or may not deem me unfit for duty. But either way you will follow their instructions. I can't protect you if you don't. Legally, there is nothing we can do. Go home. Hug a loved one. Pick up some guy and have one hell of a time. Get your mind off everything. Do something that makes you feel alive because dammit we are, and we have so much to live for and we have their memory to honor. I'm fairly certain they would be saying *oorah* right now and that's what we're going to do. Understand?"

Boyd and Callum glanced at each other then back at Kiter. They both nodded.

"Good, now call me if you need to talk. If you get low. If you have any thoughts of ending it all. You call me, do you understand?" Kiter ordered. Again, they nodded. "Good, now, I have to go and tell their families Darius and Hesler will not be coming home." With that, Kiter turned and walked out of the boardroom, his stomach in knots, the back of his neck was clammy, and his legs felt like they were on a ship rocking in the ocean.

Bypassing the elevator, he took the stairs down to the

garage and found his car. His eyes drifted to Darius' charger and the lump in this throat grew. He gripped the leather of his steering wheel and fought the tears until it hurt, then his vision swam as he stared at the car whose owner would never drive it again. He remembered Darius' smile, how it lit up the room and everyone around him was helpless to not smile. He remembered Hesler's booming laugh at something he found hilarious. How they both finished each other's sentences. How they stole little glances and smiles at each other while training or listening to a brief. The inside jokes they shared over a beer. The sheer love they had for each other and everyone they met. They never met a stranger who stayed a stranger for long. The tears kept flowing as he stared at the charger sitting unused for over a week in MI6's secured parking garage.

Finally getting himself under control, Kiter wiped his face and leaned over to the glove compartment. He pulled out his tablet. Unsanctioned meant he had some leeway and he'd be damned if he let Darius' and Hesler's parents not know how brave they were. Turning on the tablet, he found the folder he was looking for, a private one on his personal cloud account. He scrolled past the files marked *Falstaff, Boyd* and *O'Grady, Callum,* and found the one marked for Darius and Hesler. Darius always went by his last name because his first name was a family name and he hated it. *Darius, Winstone and Hesler, Richard.* Opening the folder, he clicked on the sole video for them both and hit play.

"Hey mum, hey dad," Hesler began. *"It's us."*

"Your favorite sons," Darius added with a smile and a wave.

"So, listen, we decided to join this amazing new team

and we can't tell you a lot about it," Hesler went on.

"You'll never hear much about it," Darius added.

"But it's incredible. The missions we get to go on will really mean something. They'll actually help."

"We're changing the world," Darius said with a glance at Hesler. *"We're beyond happy. And our boss is pretty badass."*

Kiter chuckled through his wet eyes.

"Yeah, he's like this soldier whisperer, I don't know. We're happy." Hesler took Darius' hand and locked eyes with him. *"But it's dangerous."*

"And if you're hearing this," Darius looked back at the camera. *"Then... we're..."*

"Dead," Hesler finished.

They were quiet for a long time. *"Wow,"* Darius' eyes shimmered a little. *"It's pretty sobering to say those words. But just know no matter what happened, it was worth it. I love what I do. I love being with Hes. This life... wow. What a gift."*

"We never want you to think we take that gift for granted, so we have a little surprise for you." Hesler lifted his hand entwined with Darius'. *"We couldn't wait to be married so when we went on vacation, we didn't just get engaged. We're married."*

Tears flowed down Kiter's eyes.

"Surprise," Darius grinned, and they leaned over to kiss each other showing their left hands with the rings. *"I love this man more than life and if one of us died, just know the other wasn't too far behind."*

"We can't say it was painless," Hesler said. *"But there would be no greater pain than living this life without this man by my side. I want you to know how much I love him."* They

looked at each other, tears in both their eyes. *"And I wouldn't want to be without him. So,"* Hesler cleared his throat and looked back at the camera. *"Mum, Dad."*

"Mum, Dad," Darius said too.

"Please don't worry about us. We're together as always. We love you."

"Remember the happy times," Darius said. *"The boating trip where my arse got sunburnt,"* he chuckled.

"The crazy skiing accident where I pulled a groin muscle and walked like grandma for two weeks," he laughed that booming laugh Kiter remembered.

"Remember us how we want to be remembered."

"And don't be sad. We're not. It was an amazing life. And we have you to thank for that."

"We love you," Darius said.

"Always," Hesler added then smiled slightly and leaned forward to turn off the camera.

Chapter Thirteen

Rhys pulled out a second beer from his fridge as the latest episode of his favorite sci-fi fantasy show was on commercial. The episode was good so far, if not a little off script from the book. He glanced at his bookshelf seeing the old, cracked spine of the paperback as he made his way back to the half-eaten bowl of popcorn and M&Ms on his coffee table. He let out a contented sigh as he sat back down. The rain's pitter-patter was the only sound apart from street noise. He hoped Collins' boys' game hadn't gotten washed out, but he hoped more that Sweet hadn't gone.

One night, long ago when he and Sweet were simply coworkers and Rhys wasn't his boss, they had gone out to the pub, got slightly inebriated and admitted their darkest secrets to each other. Rhys's being Kiter and Sweet's being how he was in love with his best friend Gabe Collins, the married straight-as-an-arrow Sergeant. Since then, Rhys had taken an interest in Sweet like a brother. They were a few years apart with Rhys being older, but he always watched out for him. Collins was oblivious of course as most men were but ever since he joined Rhys' team, he had shown his support as an ally and even took on some homophobic bullies. Of course, that didn't help Sweet's infatuation with him.

Half a mind to pick up his phone to text Sweet to check in, he was surprised to see a missed text from him from five minutes ago.

Sweet: Hey boss, think I got into some bad shrimp or something. Anyway, it's coming out of both ends. I won't be in tomorrow unless you absolutely need me.

Rhys typed back quickly.

Rhys: Not a problem, you take care of yourself. If you need me to bring over some soup, tea, or meds, let me know. Text me tomorrow if you can't make it in Wednesday.

Sweet had never called off so he must have been in pretty bad shape. When no text came through, Rhys hoped he was resting and set his phone down. Popping the tab on his beer, he unmuted the television when the show came back on and watched uninterrupted. As the credits rolled and the preview for the next week's episode ran, Rhys had a contented grin on his face. It was a good episode.

Standing, he took his two empty beer cans and what little remained of the popcorn and M&Ms to the kitchen. He washed the popcorn bowl and set it on the rack to dry, then turned out the kitchen lights. It was only 2100 and he wasn't overly tired, but he had a date with a good book and his bed. But just as he started toward his room, eager for the next chapter or three of the new fantasy he had purchased, the bell rang, and someone knocked at his door.

Confused but curious as to who would be calling on him so late, he headed over and opened the door. The sight that met him nearly stopped his heart.

"I'm sorry," Kiter sobbed. "I didn't know where else to go."

Instinct took over and Rhys pulled him over the threshold and into his arms. Kiter held on tightly and wept into his neck. Rhys' mind raced. Something had happened obviously, but to whom? Was he hurt? He felt whole and hearty. Did something happen to his family? His mother or father? He had an older brother, but he was in Gloucester surely nothing had happened to him or his wife and kids. But something caused Kiter to weep so hard it hurt Leo's chest just hearing him. He held him for several minutes, no other sound in the apartment except the rain outside and his clock ticking.

After five minutes, Leo rubbed his hand up and down Kiter's back. "Hey, hey, you'll make yourself sick. Come on. Come into the living room. Let me get you something to drink." A whisky would calm him. Kiter didn't argue, he shuffled his way into the living room and Rhys sat him down in his most comfortable chair, turned on the gas fireplace as Kiter was wet through and shivering. He hurried to his bedroom and grabbed a clean dry undershirt and a pair of joggers. Kiter stood when Rhys came back and stared at the change of clothes.

"You're not prudish now, are you?" Rhys asked.

"No, just..."

"Come on, off with it."

Kiter swallowed hard but pulled off his shirt. Rhys tried

not to stare but Sommerset was always a handsome man and though he wasn't as defined as he used to be, he was still fit and caused Rhys' mouth to water remembering how that chest tasted and felt on top of him.

Kiter hesitated when he reached for his belt. His eyes searched Rhys' face.

"It's fine. Come on."

Eventually naked, Kiter grabbed the joggers and tugged them on. Once dressed, Kiter thanked him, and Rhys poured two tumblers of whisky. He handed one to Kiter who looked exhausted. Leo sat on the couch across from him.

"What happened, Somm?" He asked gently.

Kiter's tear-drunk gaze fell on him. "I like hearing that again."

Rhys ignored the pull in his chest at his soft words. "What happened?" He asked again.

"I... I fucked up."

"How?"

Then Kiter began a story that broke Rhys' heart. Being a leader of his own team, Rhys knew the pain Kiter was enduring and desperately wanted to help him, but he knew Kiter had to go through it alone. The best way out was always through according to Robert Frost. And a best friend is the one who listened without judgement. So, Rhys listened. He listened allowing Kiter to get angry, be emotional, didn't stop the guilt he felt, and refilled his whisky glass a couple times. It was well past midnight the next time Rhys glanced at the clock. Kiter had paused his story just as he was about to tell him the parent's reaction to the video. Rhys could imagine that was difficult. Kiter finished the whisky in his glass and unfortunately, Rhys's glance at the clock wasn't subtle enough. Kiter looked to his left to see what he was looking at. When he read the time, he flinched.

"God, I'm sorry, Rhys. I didn't mean to be so long winded."

"No, no, you needed a release of emotions, don't worry about it."

"I should go," Kiter stood and promptly fell back into the chair. "Sorry," he slurred and blinked up at him. "Got to get my feet under me."

"You probably shouldn't drive," Rhys said and helped him stand.

"I'll be fine," Kiter waved him off. "I'll get home and sleep it off."

"No, Somm, you really shouldn't drive," *and dammit, neither should I.* Rhys looked into his empty glass. Then he said something he never expected to say. "You can stay here for the night."

Kiter blinked away the buzz he had and stared at Rhys. "Stay... here...?" He questioned. He had been about to say he'd get a cab or even a ride-share, but Rhys' words stopped him dead in his tracks.

"Just for tonight," Rhys clarified. "I don't want you driving. You could hurt someone."

"Right..." he nodded, though his brain was foggy. "Right." His eyes landed on the worn leather sofa. "If you wouldn't mind giving me a blanket, I'll stay here on the sofa."

Rhys looked behind him and grimaced. *Does he want me on the floor or something? Fine. I don't care.* "Or I could just stay right here. Don't want to put you out."

"No, it's not that. It's just the sofa's not very comfortable. The tufting can dig into your back. I've been meaning to throw the old thing away and get a newer one, but haven't," Rhys said.

"Oh, cheers, but I'll be fine. I've slept in worse places," Kiter said. "I was a soldier, you know."

"It would work," Rhys was muttering to himself. "And we're both adults."

"What?" Kiter asked.

Rhys turned to him with wide eyes. "I was just thinking... I have a king bed. Plenty of room. And we're both adults. It's not like we haven't shared a bed before."

And images he shouldn't be thinking of filled his mind. An image of Leo's face as he came, how the red blush extended down his pale chest, the carefree way he threw his head back as Kiter went down on him. The sounds he made as Kiter entered him slowly.

"Somm, Somm," Rhys waved in front of his face. He shook himself out of the memories. "You all right?"

"Yeah, yeah, fine," Kiter consciously had to breathe slowly to calm himself down.

"I mean, if you don't want to share, the recliner is the best alternative. I've fallen asleep there before."

"No, no, it's fine," Kiter hurriedly said. "I mean, king size bed, like you said. We're adults. And I know my limits with you. It's fine."

"All right, good," Rhys stated and walked toward a doorway. "I usually sleep with the television on. Will that bother you?"

Kiter froze, and even through his slightly drunk haze, it

dawned on him, it would be the first time they shared a bed in nearly twenty years. "You used to hate any type of light on, as I recall."

Rhys took a deep breath, his tired eyes falling on him. "A lot can happen in twenty years." Without another word, Rhys turned and walked into the bedroom. Kiter followed slowly.

The bedroom was dark, with deep grey walls, a floor to ceiling window overlooking the Thames with a great view of King Edward VII Memorial Park which was completely dark. The furniture was heavy with dark mahogany wood frames and pewter hardware. The bed's comforter set matched the walls with two white pillows accenting the place. It smelled like him too. Fiery with a hint of spice. Kiter breathed deeply, enjoying the scent. Then an image of Boyd in that space, in that bed, riding Rhys or under him, hit him out of the blue.

"Did you have sex with Boyd in this bed?" He blurted out.

Rhys stopped moving pillows from the bed to the chair. Silence lingered for a long moment until Rhys pulled the sheets and comforter down. "Not sure how that's any of your business. But yes. I've had sex with several men in this bed. If that bothers you, the recliner is always available. But I should warn you, I've had sex there too." Leo pulled off his t-shirt exposing the expanse of chest beneath. He had always been a handsome man and grew into his body by eighteen, bulking up and defining his muscles as only weights could transform a gangly kid who was a master at martial arts. Even in the military, he had an impressive physique, but the abs were less defined now and his back had more freckles on it than Kiter remembered. He looked... the best he ever looked, and all Kiter wanted to do was smooth his hands across Rhys' body like he was his again. He wanted to trace the line of his stomach with his tongue and suck love bites across his neck and chest.

"Kiter, Kiter," Rhys' voice shook him out of his thoughts and his stare down with Rhys' body. "You all right?"

"Mmhmm," he answered then looked up at him. "Bathroom?"

"Through there."

Kiter hurried out of the room and closed the bathroom door behind him. Gripping the edge of the sink as if his life depended on it, he took three deep breaths before looking up at his reflection in the mirror.

"Get it together, Sommerset," he berated himself. "He doesn't want you like that. He doesn't deserve to be treated like shit and have you expect things from him. He's being nice and wants to help you. Don't screw this up."

He washed his hands and patted his face with the damp cloth. Walking out of the bathroom, he steeled himself against the vision that awaited him. No surprise, Rhys sat up in bed, shirtless flicking through the channels on the television. He glanced up at him and Kiter saw the unease filling his eyes. A gentleman would bow out. A good guy would say *I'll sleep on the couch.* A friend would not put his friend through that. But Kiter professed to neither being a gentleman nor a good guy and they were far from friends.

"I usually sleep nude," Kiter said. Rhys' eyes widened. "But would it be okay if I wore just my pants?" Rhys nodded quickly and looked away, apparently finding a commercial for hemorrhoid ointment fascinating.

Kiter stripped out of his shirt and jeans to his grey briefs and crawled under the sheets. They had lain like that so many times before it was old habit, but the nervous tension coursing through them was new. Rhys was right, the bed was large enough for them to sleep and not touch. Kiter wasn't sure if he was relieved or disappointed by that fact.

There was an awkward silence as they both stared at the television, currently on another commercial, that time for male assistance in the bedroom.

"Commercials these days, huh?" Kiter tried to lift the mood. "I mean if it's not sex, it's drinking, if it's not sex or drinking, it's what to do after sex and drinking."

Rhys chuckled. "I mean, think about it, sex and drinking... they know their audience at least."

Kiter laughed. "Yeah, I guess you're right." They glanced at each other, their smiles slowly fading then looked away. More awkward silence descended.

"Do you have to work tomorrow? Or could we maybe, I don't know, get breakfast?" Kiter offered.

"I have to work," Rhys answered not looking at him.

"Oh, right, yeah, of course," Kiter looked down and toyed with the edge of the sheet.

They were quiet again. "I'll try not to wake you when I leave," Rhys said.

"No, that's okay. I'll get out of your hair. Thanks for letting me crash here tonight."

"You were in no state to drive," Rhys answered.

"Still, you could have kicked me out. I'm sure you wanted to."

Rhys said nothing for a long while until he leaned over to turn off the light on the nightstand and stayed on his side. "Goodnight, Somm."

Kiter held in his sigh and rolled to his side, his back facing Rhys' back. "Goodnight, Rhys," he said and closed his eyes.

Chapter Fourteen

Rhys wasn't sure what had woken him, but he opened his eyes and was met with Kiter's sleeping face. Sometime during the night, they had both turned over and faced each other. But what surprised Rhys even more was Kiter had his hand resting on Rhys' hip and Rhys held Kiter's other arm cradling it almost like a pillow. Carefully removing both, Rhys watched as Kiter's face contorted. At first, it looked like confusion, then it morphed into pain. Kiter groaned and whimpered. His breathing picked up and he rolled to his back.

"Dar... Hes... no," he breathed.

Rhys' heart squeezed. Darius and Hesler, the two men Kiter told him he lost on the mission.

"Shh shh shh, it's all right," Rhys soothed a hand over Kiter's chest. He calmed almost instantly. "I'm here, you're all right, Somm."

"Rhys," he moaned. "Rhys, no, I... I'm sorry. Don't leave me, please. I'm sorry."

"Shh, rest, it's all right."

"Rhys, Rhys," he breathed softly and settled. Rhys watched him for a long moment. He was deluding himself if he thought for one moment he was over him. Silly, he knew. But it was true. Sommerset Kiter was the love of his life and even though with all the good came all the bad memories, pain, hurt, anger; the good overshadowed it all. They weren't perfect. But they had love, respect, compatibility. Then Kiter had to ruin it all.

Maybe it was unfair of him. Maybe Rhys looked at it wrong. They were each other's firsts, their only, but was it unfair to have expected him to only want him for the rest of his days and Geoff Ainsley had been young and more than willing... *but it wasn't unfair, dammit.* They had been in a committed relationship and in Rhys' mind, Kiter was enough for him. Always had been. Always would be. So why did Kiter not feel the same? Rhys fell to his back and huffed. The argument they had before he shipped out, had been over an inconsequential matter. Rhys couldn't even remember what it was about, but he said things in anger he could never take back and he heard things said in anger he could never unhear. Then he saw things he could never unsee such as Kiter in their bed with Geoff, the man he was still friends with. Would he go back to him? Would Rhys come home one day and find them in bed again? Or even a threesome with Geoff's boyfriend, Peter. How did he knew beyond a shadow of a doubt Kiter would be loyal this time? And would that shadow of his infidelity hang over their relationship forever?

Rhys' headache that always started behind his eyes since his fall years ago began again. He was working himself up.

"What has you thinking so hard?" Kiter's voice came from beside him. He looked over.

"How long have you been awake?"

"Long enough to see you hurting yourself thinking so hard." Kiter leaned up on his elbow and looked down at him. His face and bare chest cast in moonlight making his skin glow with an otherworldly light. "Had a bad dream which woke me up. What's wrong?"

Rhys' hand had a mind of its own and he reached up to caress Kiter's face. They both froze for a moment, then Kiter leaned into the touch.

"What did we argue about?" Rhys finally asked. Kiter's brow furrowed. "Before I left, twenty years ago," Rhys clarified. "We argued about something. What was it?"

Kiter took a moment to think, then licked his lips. "I... I don't remember. I remember I was upset about something. We said things to each other that hurt but deep down, I knew you didn't mean it and it was just a way to argue. I remember you saying if that's how I felt, maybe we should take a break. I remember that was the moment my heart broke and I yelled at you. I said things I regret and can never take back."

"You called me a whore. Your little bitch."

Tears glistened in Kiter's eyes. "I remember. I didn't mean it. I was angry but that's no excuse. Then you left. I didn't know where we stood. I didn't think we were even together anymore because of what we said to each other. I hated you for leaving and not clearing the air. Then Geoff came into my life. I did try to resist him. But my anger at you surfaced when I remembered you saying you didn't want to be with a controlling freak like me. And I allowed our physical relationship. The first time I was with him, I nearly threw up thinking I had cheated on you. And I was his teacher. It was wrong. I hated myself. But you and I. We were... I didn't know what, and selfishly, I took what I thought I wanted, and that was Geoff, for a short time at least... But I never loved him like I love you. I was always so sick afterward. As much as I cared for him, he wasn't you and I knew it every time. It wasn't fair to anyone. We were only together a couple months. But when you came home, I knew I had lost you completely. I saw the moment your pain and betrayal turned into hatred, and I am so sorry I ever did it. I'm so sorry for what I said to you. I should never have let you leave without clearing the air. I... was just so angry at you. And I can't remember why."

Rhys nodded slowly. "You were my first and only for a long time. The stupidly in love part of me thought we'd be together forever but... when I left, I didn't know what we were either. We never talked while I was away. I thought maybe you were still angry. I had offers. Guys and women wanting to sleep with me, but I didn't. I didn't know what we were. If we were a couple or not. I was so confused. But when I got back, I wanted to make amends but was so hurt by what you did with Geoff. I guess... maybe we can leave it to youth, inexperience, and miscommunication."

"I would like that. And I make this promise to you. I will work every day to prove my contrition. I will try to be worthy of your forgiveness."

With a sigh, Rhys nodded. "Me too."

Kiter was quiet for a long moment, then took Rhys' hand that he had placed back on his stomach. Folding his hand around

Rhys', Kiter twisted their hands to interlock their fingers.

"One thing I have learned from Darius' and Hesler's deaths is we aren't guaranteed tomorrow. And I would rather spend what little time I have left on this earth with the man I love more than life itself. I don't know how you feel, I never could ask you to forget my faults, but I am here. I want to be with you and you alone. I'm sorry for all my part in our pain. I never could call you those words. You are not a whore, never were and as far as being my little..." Kiter looked away looking physically pained to remember the word he said. "I hurt you so badly and I can never take it back. I can never heal the hurt I caused, but I would like to prove to you I'm not that man anymore. I love you more than words can say. Dare I hope, that maybe, in time, you could come to see me as you once did? Perhaps even grow to love me once more?"

Rhys' breath faltered. "I've never stopped." With no more words, Rhys reached up and captured the back of Kiter's neck. Tugging him down, Somm met him halfway and pressed his lips to Rhys in a kiss. The deep moan Kiter let out gave Rhys a chance to move forward. Their tongues dueled and their lips moved together. Kissing Kiter again was like being able to breathe after nearly drowning. The hurt was still there, but the joy of life raced through him. Rhys lay back down bringing Kiter with him. The press of his chest against Rhys', the feel of his hands on his sides, the press of his erection against his thigh was everything he was missing in his life. It was perfect. He was finally home. After nearly twenty years floating around, he was finally home.

Kiter reached down and outlined Rhys' cock with his fingers.

"Let me make you feel good, baby." Kiter pulled away just slightly.

Rhys grabbed him back and kissed him but nodded. "Yes, please."

Kiter dove under the waistband of Rhys' underwear and gripped his erection. Rhys let out a pleasured gasp.

"Fuck." Rhys arched into him and panted. "Somm." He gasped and swallowed hard.

"Rhys, baby, god I fucking missed you."

"I... missed you too."

Kiter pulled Rhys' pants down and hooked the waistband under his balls. The air hit his flesh and made him shiver. Kiter pulled away and started sucking marks into his skin at his neck and chest. Then lower still. He bit the softer skin at his middle and made his way down. Rhys allowed himself to just feel.

The pleasure coursing through him was overwhelming. The moment Somm's lips closed over the head of Rhys' cock, all other thought fled.

"Fuuuuuck," he moaned. "Somm, Somm, aye fuck."

Somm sucked and licked his way down his length. Panting, Rhys' finger dove into Somm's hair as he arched into the sensation. Sommerset didn't tease him and Rhys was thankful. He was too pent up to make it last.

Somm popped off his cock and licked the underside vein while sucking a finger into his mouth. He lowered that finger to Rhys' balls, toyed there for a moment before lowering further to his entrance. Looking up as he sucked a bruise into the crease between Rhys' thigh and groin, Rhys nodded and Sommerset slowly worked his finger into Rhys' entrance. As soon as he breached Rhys' hole, he moaned slow and low. Pumping his finger in and out of Rhys, Sommerset went lower and sucked and nipped at Rhys' balls.

"Fuck, Somm, please."

Sommerset didn't play. He found Rhys' prostate and pressed firmly as he sucked hard on the head of Rhys' cock. Rhys groaned and let go, spilling down Somm's throat. He flew.

"Fuck," he moaned when he returned to earth. He heard Somm grunt and looked down seeing his man stroking his cock faster and faster chasing his own climax.

With a lethargic hand, Rhys reached down. The moment he touched Somm's cock, all focus returned, and he stroked his lover the way he remembered he liked. Somm gasped and panted, leaning forward and resting his head on Rhys' shoulder, just feeling.

"Let go, Somm. I'll catch you."

With those words and deep guttural groan, Sommerset spilled over Rhys' hand.

The shrill sound of his phone echoing through the room startled him. They both panted for air but shared a look of joy mixed with a little trepidation. Somm placed his forehead against Rhys' and they giggled... giggled like little school girls. After a beat, Rhys leaned over to grab his phone on the nightstand as Somm slowly stood and went to the bathroom. Running water sounded next as Rhys checked his phone. Seeing a missed call from *Collins,* he furrowed his brow and looked back up at Kiter who came back with a damp cloth in his hand. Kiter smiled softly at him. The warm cloth wiped over Rhys, cleaning him of the sticky release.

"Do you need to call him back?" Kiter asked, indicating

the phone.

"No, I'm sure if it's important, he'll leave a message."

They were quiet for a long moment. "Thank you," Kiter finally said softly.

"For what?"

"For giving me hope and a glimpse of happiness."

Rhys' lips turned up in a gentle smile. He pulled Kiter back down and rested his forehead against his again. "Thank you for showing up here tonight. And for finally talking it out."

Kiter chuckled. "Only took us twenty years."

Rhys agreed and grinned. "Let's not wait twenty more to do this again." He took Kiter's hand and guided it down his body to the part of him that was spent and twitching. Kiter gifted him with a salacious grin.

"Haven't lost your touch," he moaned. But before Kiter could do more than tease him again, his phone rang once more. Rhys wanted to smack it but looking over at the name. *Collins* again showed in white. His brows furrowed and he instantly grabbed it. Grateful Kiter seemed to understand and pulled away slightly. Rhys answered.

"Gabe? What's wrong?"

"Boss, I'm with Sweet. We need you," Collins said raggedly over the phone.

Rhys was up and out of bed before he spoke again. "What happened?"

"I don't know. I had a bad feeling when he didn't show up at the boys' game. I called him, he didn't answer, and my texts were delivered but not read. I couldn't sleep so I came over," Collins explained. Rhys glanced at the clock and put him on speaker as he grabbed his shirt.

"What happened?" He pressed again.

"He didn't answer the door at first, so I was gonna use my key, but he finally did. Boss, he's been beaten something fierce."

"Beaten?" Rhys demanded pausing and locking eyes with Kiter who was out of bed and pulling on his jeans. "He told me he had a stomach problem."

"He's bad off, boss. He refuses to go to the hospital. What do I do?"

"I'm on my way. Keep him still, get a cold compress on the worst spots."

"He's... oh god, he's hurt boss. I swear when I find the guy who did this, he'll wish he never laid a finger on him," Collins said.

"Has he said who did it?" Rhys asked pulling on a jacket and moving through his house to the entryway.

"Nothing, he hasn't said a damn thing. He refuses to tell me."

"Okay okay, I'm on my way."

"Hurry, please," Collins begged.

"I'm leaving now," Rhys hung up and looked over at Kiter. "I have to go."

"I heard," Kiter walked over to him and pulled him into him. "Anything I can do?"

"I don't think so, but thanks for offering."

"Of course," he pulled back and cupped his face. "Listen, I'll get going, I know you've got to go in to work tomorrow and I don't want to hang around here uninvited."

"You're welcome to, but you're place probably has better cable."

Kiter grinned. "You'll have to come and see for yourself one of these days."

"I don't even know where you live," Rhys replied, then drew his eyebrows together.

"You will," Kiter said lifting his chin to look at him. "Be careful, let me know how things go."

Rhys nodded and grabbed his keys and helmet. He had gotten a motorcycle instead of a new car when Boyd had confirmed his was stripped for parts.

"Hey," Kiter pulled him back once more and slipped his arms around his waist, settling his hands on his ass, a move he had done a thousand times and yet was still so foreign. "I..." he swallowed. Rhys had a distinct impression of what he wanted to say but didn't. "Be careful, yeah?" He kissed him quickly and let him go. Rhys squeezed his arm in thanks and hurried out the door. He was certain the gravity of what he had just done with Kiter would crash over him soon, but he hoped it wasn't until after he got Sweet to hospital.

Chapter Fifteen

Rhys knocked on Sweet's front door and waited. After about fifteen seconds, Collins opened the door. He looked as ragged as he had sounded on the phone. His hair was askew, and his clothing was rumpled.

"Boss! Thank god, you're here." Collins tugged him inside and shut the door.

"Has he said anything?" Rhys asked.

"Finally, yeah, he said he was attacked on the way home from the pub," Collins said as Rhys pulled off his jacket. "I don't believe him."

"Why?"

Collins shrugged. "I know him. I know his tells. He's lying."

Rhys stared at him for a long moment. Collins and Sweet were best friends, had been since Sweet was sixteen, twenty years ago. Recently, Rhys shook his head, Collins had been acting more possessive of him. Sweet would talk about a date he went on and Collins would go silent and cold for a while then say the man didn't deserve Sweet. It was strange.

Not to mention Rhys had seen him staring at Sweet's ass on more than one occasion. But Rhys had little time to ponder on it, he needed to see his friend. "Take me to him."

Collins nodded and hurried through the flat. Sweet's place was a swanky townhouse in a good neighborhood. He had told Rhys the first time he had come over for cards that he came from money and the place was his parents old place when they had moved back to the British Virgin Islands nearly ten years ago. The decorations were tasteful and yet Rhys saw the subtle hints placed around the area showing Sweet's two personalities. The flamboyant out and proud personal life and the more subdued, badass cop he was professionally.

Rhys followed Collins through the main room to the master bedroom. The lights were dim, and the television was on low. Sweet looked up from his phone as they came into the room and Rhys grimaced. Sweet's lip was busted, his left eye, jaw, and forehead were heavily bruised, and he held his right arm close over his stomach as if it hurt. Rhys saw the bruising on his bare torso and a redness on his right shoulder that looked like rug burn.

"Boss," he said, his voice gravelly and low. "You didn't have to come all this way. I was gonna rest tomorrow... well, today I suppose, and make it in tomorrow," Sweet explained.

"Nigel," Rhys replied walking over and sitting on the bed by his knees. "I'm not happy with you for lying to me. You should have told me the truth."

"I know, I'm sorry. I didn't want a fuss." He shifted, and a pained expression crossed his milk chocolate features. Collins raced to him to help but Sweet waved him off.

"There's no fuss," Rhys said watching Collins move around the bed like a mother hen. "But we need to know what happened."

Sweet shook his head. "I got jumped, nothing more."

Rhys and Collins locked eyes for a moment then looked back at him. "When?"

"Earlier."

"Where?"

"Out."

"Did you report it to the police?"

"I am the police," Sweet said. "Besides I didn't get a good look at the guy."

"Were you out on a date?" Rhys asked and Collins stiffened beside him.

"Is that why you didn't tell me?" Collins demanded. "Did a guy do this to you? Did he hurt you? Did he rape you?"

"Woah, easy," Rhys placed a hand on his arm which Collins promptly shook off.

"Did he?" Collins demanded.

"Gabe," Sweet stopped him. "No, I'm fine. And no, it wasn't a date."

"A hookup?" Rhys asked.

"No, okay?" Sweet was exasperated. "No romantic or sexual hookup did this to me, okay? I wasn't raped, I was beaten up by a guy who didn't like that I was gay, okay? Happy now?"

"So it was a hate crime," Rhys surmised.

"My word against his, doesn't matter."

"It matters to me!" Collins nearly shouted.

"Why? Why does anything matter to you?" Sweet shouted back.

"Hey, hey, come on, Gabe, he doesn't need that. Nigel, he is worried about you." Rhys stood and placed a hand on Collins' chest. "Go get some water for him." When Collins wouldn't drop Sweet's gaze, Rhys stood directly in front of him cutting off his line of sight. "Now." Collins looked up at him and huffed then left the room. Rhys sat back down. "Nigel, what happened?"

Nigel closed his eyes. "Swear to me you won't tell him?" His voice was low almost as if he expected Collins to be listening at the door.

"I swear."

Sweet nodded and took a shallow breath. "Bethel." He said softly.

"What?" Rhys breathed. "When?"

"Just after you left. Apparently, he had overheard us talking and me saying how much I care for Collins. He accused me of spreading my *disease* and turning straight guys. He called me... so many names both for my sexuality and my skin color I refuse to repeat them."

"I can surmise," Rhys placed a hand on Sweet's wrist resting on his stomach. "You need to get checked out. He's not very smart, but Bethel has some bulk on him."

"I held my own."

"I'm sure you did," Rhys encouraged. "But he's got a few pounds on you. He's dumb but big and strong. If he got you in the stomach, you could have a couple broken ribs."

"I don't feel like it," Sweet said. "I've had them before, and this doesn't feel the same. I'm just tired. I want to sleep."

"Then let's get you to hospital and get something stronger than acetaminophen. I'm going to need to report this. Bethel can't get away with it."

"I threw the first punch, boss." Sweet looked away.

"You were provoked," Rhys replied.

"And it'll be my word against his."

Rhys couldn't argue with that. He was right. "Come on, let's get you checked out. Then, we can figure out what to do next."

Sweet looked down but eventually nodded. "Good. Gabe!" Rhys called. The sound of running footsteps was next. Collins raced into the room. "Get your car. We're going to hospital."

"Oh, thank god." Collins all but pushed Rhys out of the way to help Sweet stand. His grip never faltered as he helped him up. In a way, he reminded Rhys of Kiter. When he had been in the hospital after his accident, Kiter had come to visit him and help him sit up and eventually walk around. He hated when he came but never told the nurses to refuse him. Maybe even then Rhys wanted him back and didn't know how to say it. With that thought came all the revelations and memories of earlier. He itched to call Kiter, tell him what happened, but he waited. He pushed his thoughts to the back of his mind as he went around Sweet's room gathering a change of clothes into his hold all. It was chilly and Sweet was always cold, a product of being born on a Caribbean Island, so Rhys grabbed a zip up hooded sweatshirt and helped him into it before they got him to the door. Collins was helping Sweet into his car as Rhys pulled on his helmet. He took out his phone to see a text waiting for him.

Kiter: Hope everything is all right. I'm here if you need.

Thank you. For everything last night and this morning. I'm sorry our time was cut a little short, though.

Rhys chuckled, so was he.

Rhys: Everything is okay. Getting him to hospital. Depending on what they say, it might be a while. I'll have to check in later with work, but is that breakfast date still on the table? Could meet you around maybe nine?

Kiter's reply came almost immediately.

Kiter: Yes! It's still on the table. Absolutely! Just let me know if nine works. I'm off the next two weeks, as you know, so I'm open. What hospital are you taking him to? I can see what's around there.

Rhys: How about Berry's? They have good coffee cake.

Kiter: Of course they have good coffee cake... You got to have your cinnamon fix.

Rhys: You know me. Cinnamon is life.

After he sent the text he realized what he said. Kiter did know him more than anyone else.

Kiter: I'm not complaining. Cinnamon has always been your scent to me.

Rhys: Are you saying I stink? *Laughing emoji*

Kiter: I would never! Haha

Rhys: Rude

He added a second text with a winky faced emoji, so Kiter knew he was teasing. But it was true. Cinnamon was his favorite flavor of anything. It was fiery and yet flavorful. He blamed the *Leo* inside him for liking anything resembling fire. And that included playing with it. He was definitely playing with fire in his relationship with Kiter. He just hoped he wouldn't get burned again. Glancing back at Collins and Sweet, Collins was hurrying over to his driver's side and gave him a nod. They were ready.

Rhys: Gotta go. Collins is ready to drive Sweet to hospital. I'll let you know how it goes.

Kiter: Okay, be careful.

Rhys smiled and sent an *I will* text before turning his phone to sleep and putting it in the pocket of his bike. Signaling to Collins he was ready, he kicked his bike in gear, and drove down Sweet's street toward the main road.

Chapter Sixteen

Kiter waited at Berry's, a coffee cake and bagel breakfast sandwich on the table along with his black coffee and Rhys' cinnamon dolce latte. He was early but had finished his workout and showered before making his way to the breakfast café. He wanted to be nearby in case Rhys needed him. When he had gotten Rhys' text that the doctors had cleared Sweet of any major internal injuries and diagnosed only sprains and bruises, he had breathed a sigh of relief. Rhys didn't need the pain that came with losing a member of his team. Rhys had followed up ten minutes later that he would be able to meet him in twenty.

That was eighteen minutes ago, and Kiter had to consciously stop his knee from bouncing. The location was different, but the setting was the same as the last time they had met at a café, and it had ended so horribly. He wasn't a praying man, but he sent up a silent prayer to whatever deity was listening that all went well that day.

The bells jingled over the door and Kiter looked up. Rhys was walking over to him in those biker boots, dark jeans, and black t-shirt with leather jacket unzipped. God, that man was sex on legs. The smile he wore was soft but playful and it took Kiter's breath.

"Hey handsome," Rhys said when he got close enough and leaned down placing a kiss on Kiter's surprised mouth. "Mm, thank you. I can smell the cinnamon from here."

Kiter let out the breath he was holding and with it, his cheeks began to hurt with how wide his smile was. He schooled his features to be less of the eager teenager he felt.

"How's Sweet?" He asked as Rhys sat down across from him.

"Recuperating," Rhys said taking his mug of coffee and a deep sniff. "Mm, smells amazing."

"I should know your order. Hasn't changed since we were teens."

"What can I say? I like something, I hold on to it." He took a sip and let out the sexiest moan Kiter had heard since... earlier that morning.

"Did he... ehm, heh," his voice cracked, and he let out a chuckle when he saw the faux innocent look on Rhys' face. "You know exactly what you're doing to me, don't you?"

"I don't know what you mean," he grinned as he cut into his coffee cake. Bringing the fork to his lips, he took the bite but let his tongue swipe out to lick the bottom of the fork. Kiter squirmed as his jeans were suddenly tight.

"Damn you," he shook his head. Rhys chuckled then leaned back, their play time was over. "Did he tell you what happened?"

"Yes," Rhys answered. "It was a hate crime."

"Because?"

"Well because he is a gay black man from the Virgin Islands. That's a twofer for some homophobic racist."

"Does he know who attacked him?" Kiter asked taking a drink of his bitter black coffee.

"Yes, but there's nothing we can do."

"Why?"

"Well, because the man who did it is the super's nephew and on my team." Rhys took another drink.

"Shit," Kiter answered.

"He told me in confidence so don't mention it. Collins would go batshit."

"The man attacked his boyfriend. He has every right. Trust me. You work with this guy? Has he ever laid a hand on you?" Kiter demanded.

"One, thank you for your concern, but I can take care of myself. Two, Collins isn't Sweet's boyfriend. Collins is married and straight. They're best friends."

"Sure sounded like he was a concerned partner," Kiter answered, instantly calming. "And sorry, I know you can. It's just, I guess my protective instincts haven't gone away since we were kids, huh?"

"I always appreciated your protective instincts. But we aren't kids anymore. I can take care of myself, aye?"

"Yeah, of course," Kiter answered. "Sorry." Rhys gave him a genuine soft smile. "Are you going to talk to your Super?"

Rhys sighed. "I have to, she wants me to come in. Probably to tell me Sweet is suspended."

"Why would he be suspended?"

"He threw the first punch. The man is an incredible cop. He's able to blend in in a crowd. He's an actor. He can do at least six different accents, speaks three languages. He's amazing. But he's not as strong as others. He's sensitive, rightly so, to many slurs. He's had to live most of his life hearing people's judgment of him based on his skin tone and orientation. He first met Collins when he was getting bullied at sixteen. Collins stopped the bullies. So, I suppose that's where they both are when it comes to someone hurting him."

"Sounds like a great friend."

"He is," Rhys agreed. They paused.

"I sense a but there?"

Rhys sighed and leaned forward. "I don't know. I just am a little concerned. They have always had this connection, but recently, it's gotten more and more... heated. Not in a bad or angry way, more like a..."

"Sexual tension?"

"Yeah," Rhys agreed. "I don't know. Maybe I'm crazy."

"If you feel it, you're not crazy. You know your men. But you said Collins is straight?"

"Doesn't stop him from staring at Sweet's arse in the showers."

Kiter's eyes widened and his brows rose as he leaned back. "Seriously?"

Rhys nodded. "Caught him looking yesterday."

"Damn."

"So, I don't know. It's just messing with team dynamic. And it gives guys like Bethel fodder for their fire."

"How many do you have on your team?"

"A core three, Sweet, Collins, and Bethel, but depending on the size or scope of the mission, I can call up to ten more."

"That's amazing."

"It's a good gig, just don't like the super. She's... difficult."

"I can understand that if she allows her nephew to be the way he is."

"And being such a small team, we have to be tight. Bethel hates Sweet and me because of who we find attractive. And he hates Collins because he's such a good ally. I don't know. This whole thing is a clusterfeck. It's all come down to this moment and depending on how she reacts..."

"Could you report her to her boss?"

"Maybe, but the Chief Super is too busy to take care of a minor squabble between grown ass men."

"Well, you know the position with my team is always open for you. I'm not sure where we stand yet as far as recruiting. But as soon as I know, you're welcome to be with us," Kiter offered.

Rhys looked down into his coffee and Kiter instantly recalled his words to see if he could have offended him. Then realized, he very easily could have.

"I'm sorry, I didn't mean—"

"I never apologized for how I just walked out on you and..." he glanced around. "The others."

"There's no need," Kiter said. "Rhys, it was my fault. You had every right to react the way you did. I should have told you about my involvement or had Callum do it. And I should never have sprung Boyd on you like that."

"It was just a shock. I was so hopeful that this new team was going to be great. It was going to be fun and when I didn't know everything about it, it hurt, ya ken?"

"I do, I can't say I'm sorry enough, Rhys. I was a bloody coward and didn't want the confrontation. But in doing so, I nearly lost you completely." The memory of Darius and Hesler dying entered his mind, only that time it was Rhys. "And I cannot say I'm not scared to death about the possibility of you getting hurt. I've already lost two men, but I can't stand in your way. I can't lose you when I only just got you back."

"Hey," Rhys said softly and covered Kiter's hand with his. "You're not going to lose me."

"You're the best one for the job, that's why I told Callum to recruit you. But the idea it could have been you on that beach makes my heart want to stop. I get why Hesler stayed behind. Without his husband, there was no reason to live. There was nothing for him in a world without Darius. I understand that now. I think I always have, that's why I took their deaths so hard."

"Somm," Rhys intertwined their fingers. "I appreciate that. I get why they did what they did. But we're not them. And if we do this, you have got to promise me you won't try to smother me. You won't try to control me. If we do this, it's a partnership, not a dictatorship. And you cannae stop me from doing what I know is right. Now, you can question my motives privately, together alone, but not in front of the team. I don't want to be considered as the teacher's pet simply because we're sleeping together."

Kiter's eyes widened and he swallowed hard. Rhys stopped, seeming to realize his words and chuckled. "There I go again, getting ahead of myself."

"Hey, no complaints here. Name the place and time,"

Kiter grinned.

Rhys laughed and squeezed his hand, bringing them back to seriousness. "Can you promise me that?"

"Yes," Kiter stated. "It will be so difficult if I think you're in danger, but you are right. You are an amazing soldier and officer. You have earned the right not to be questioned. I know you can take care of yourself. We're forty-two years old, I think we both are grown enough to make our own decisions, don't you?" he chuckled.

"Thank you," Rhys said. "That's all I want. And if the position is still open and if you can still recruit, I'm in."

"Boyd and all?"

"Boyd and all. Besides he was fun." With a wink, Rhys bit his lower lip and Kiter growled.

"You're not going to touch him again, do you understand? You're mine."

"Am I?" Rhys leaned back in his chair and slowly took a drink. Kiter tamped down his possessiveness.

"Shit, that was a test, wasn't it?"

"Yes, and you failed." Rhys leaned forward and kissed his cheek. "But it was cute."

Kiter breathed a laugh. "Whatever, ya nutter."

"How very adult of you," Rhys grinned.

"Shut up." He sulked and took a drink of his coffee.

Rhys laughed and leaned back. "So talk to me. Tell me how your family is. Fill me in on twenty years' worth of stories."

Kiter watched as Rhys took a bite of his coffee cake and watched him expectantly. Digging into his bagel sandwich, Kiter told him all about his brother's family and his nieces and nephews and how much he loved being an uncle. By the time they finished eating, Kiter had Rhys laughing so hard tears sprung to his eyes and he was begging for mercy. It was so good to hear him laugh, Kiter didn't want to stop but he allowed him to get his breath back after laughing at something Kiter's father had done in the care home. Rhys' phone dinged and as he wiped his eyes, he grabbed the device and looked at the text, sighing as he read it.

"Super?" Kiter asked.

"Aye," Rhys answered. "Wants me to come in. Needs to talk to me."

"Let me check something first?" Kiter asked. At Rhys' nod he pulled out his phone, and sent a text to Lester.

Kiter: What's the status? Is Charing Cross still a go? I have recruits waiting.

"Okay. I'll tell you what he says. I don't want you to quit without a backup."

"I'm good but thank you. I have enough savings to hold me over a couple months. It's just me so I don't splurge on a lot," Rhys drained his coffee and stood.

"Ehm, what about dinner?" Kiter asked standing too.

"Dinner?" Rhys looked at him.

"Yeah, can I, I mean, would it be okay if I took you to dinner? Tonight?"

Rhys paused pulling on his coat, then the corner of his lip tipped up. "Yeah, dinner sounds good."

"I'll swing by your place and pick you up?" Kiter offered. "Say, 2030?"

"2030 works."

"You still a vegetarian?" Kiter questioned.

"Have been since I was seventeen," Rhys answered.

"Though I do like the occasional fish in my diet, so not religious."

"Then I have the perfect place in mind," Kiter said walking Rhys to the door of the café after they dropped off their plates and mugs at the dish drop off. The sun had finally shown after a few days of rain, and it was glorious to stand in the warmth.

"Call me crazy, but it's almost like the rain washed away our past and the sun is shining down on us again as we start this new chapter of our lives," Rhys said.

"So poetic, Leo," Kiter winked. Even though he called him Rhys for only a couple days, it was odd to call him Leo again.

"Only for you."

Kiter took him into his arms and pulled him flush against him. "Will you miss me?"

"I won't miss your ego," Rhys' chest bounced with a laugh.

"It's a big ego," Kiter wiggled his brows suggestively.

"Not as big as others," Rhys answered.

"You wound me."

"A baby cut. I'm sure a big strong man like you can take it."

"Wanker." They chuckled and Kiter rested his hands on Rhys' ass again, as if he had done it all along. "See you tonight?"

"I look forward to it. Will we go back to my place? Or yours?"

Kiter swallowed hard. "Whatever works."

"Yours I'll need to bring a couple things, mine, I have everything in the drawers of the nightstand."

Kiter licked his lips. "Yours it is then."

Rhys' lip tipped up in a sexy smirk and a dimple popped.

"I got to go."

"Kiss me?"

"So demanding," Rhys teased but leaned down and fused his mouth to Kiter's. The kiss was heated, but being in public, they pulled back much too soon. And Rhys pulled on his helmet and straddled his motorcycle. The bike roared to life as he kicked it in gear and, with a small wave, a rev of the engine making Kiter grin, Rhys pulled away and down the road toward Scotland Yard. Kiter waited until he was out of view before taking his phone out of his pocket and dialing a number.

"What's up, baby bro? Long time," his brother answered.

"Hey Gray," he said keeping his voice light. "I need to talk to you."

"What's up?" Grayson Kiter asked.

"Rhys and I are getting back together and I'm honestly the happiest I've ever been."

"What?" Gray cheered. "That's amazing! Talk to me, how did it happen?"

"Long story, got time?"

"For this? Hell yes, I make time."

Kiter grinned and launched into the story.

Chapter Seventeen

Leo pulled into his designated parking space in the garage of his precinct. The stupid grin on his face needed to go away. He needed to be professional when he entered his boss' office but no matter what he did, he still remembered the feel of Kiter's lips and hands all over him and the smile stayed. He hadn't been happy like that in nearly two decades. His phone dinged and he pulled it out of his zipper jacket pocket as he walked.

Kiter: CCB is still a go. Dump that bitch and come to me.

He grinned and texted back.

Rhys: About to go in. Wish me luck that I don't kill anyone responsible.

Kiter: You're part of CCB now, we'll cover it up.

Laughing, he sent back a kiss emoji and put his phone on mute. As he walked toward the glass door of his super's office, he put all feelings away and simply remembered Sweet's battered body and how the man seated in the office opposite the super was responsible for his pain.

He cleared his throat and knocked on the door. "Come," she called. He opened the door and nodded to his boss.

"Ma'am," he greeted.

"Campbell, shut the door, have a seat," she said. He did and even though his hand clenched seeing Bethel, black eye and cut on his cheek, beside him, he waited. "We have an issue." She said from behind her desk. He waited. When she didn't continue, he glanced at Bethel then back at her.

"What issue is that, ma'am?" He asked.

"It appears there was an altercation between two members of your team," she said. "Were you aware?"

"I was," he answered. "I just came from Nigel Sweet's hospital room. He told me everything." He looked over at Bethel expectantly.

"That faggot probably lied," Bethel spat.

"That's all the proof I need of his issues. What happens now, ma'am? I'm assuming he's transferred to some remote region. May I recommend Scotland? He'd probably enjoy it there. No one around for miles and men large enough to take care of themselves against a little racist bigot like him."

"I ain't goin' no where."

"So eloquently put, Bethel." Rhys turned to look at his super. "What do you need from me? A signature on transfer papers? I'm happy to do whatever is necessary."

"It's not that simple," she answered. "I have reviewed the tape and it shows Sergeant Sweet threw the first punch."

"That's because your nephew spewed such vile filth that

he had no reservation in getting him to shut up. Now, I suggest we do this the easiest way and on the transfer papers state irreconcilable differences as the reason for his transfer."

"That faggot had it coming. Spreading his disease."

"Is that the sort of language you want associated with your department, ma'am?"

"Stan, shut it," she said to her nephew. Then looked at Rhys. "I will decide what I will and will not associate with, Commander Campbell."

"With all due respect, ma'am, if someone on my team called you a heartless bitch I would expect their transfer to go through without delay. Simply because you are, shouldn't matter. But it appears Sergeant Bethel is to be given a free pass because of politics and who he's related to. I will not stand for it. This man insulted someone I care very much about and if he is not suitably punished, I cannot be held accountable for my actions. Nor that of my team."

"Are you making threats, Commander?" She demanded.

"No, no threat, ma'am, it's up to you what part of my statement is untrue." Rhys shrugged. "This is not the first time this has happened. He has spoken in a very derogatory manner about not just Sweet but of myself that even straight members of my team have heard his hatred and defended us."

"Us, see Auntie?" Bethel pounced. "There's no way to have a fair judgment when he classifies himself as a wounded party."

Rhys wanted to snap off the fingers he used as air quotes around *wounded party* and shove them up his arse.

"I am merely explaining that this behavior which goes against our very foundation as an organization is not new," Rhys said. "Sweet may have thrown the first punch, but he is in hospital with injuries sustained after he was knocked down. Bethel kept beating him, kicking him I believe is what Sweet said, after he was down. That sort of behavior should trump any first punch throw, in a very obviously provoked attack. Sweet came to me just yesterday saying he didn't feel safe around Sergeant Bethel and now his actions have proven that to be true."

"That fucker hit me first!" Bethel shouted.

"Oh yes, and I'm sure you stopped once he was down. And I'm sure you stopped when he asked you to."

"He's spreading his disease. I heard you two talking about turning Collins! It's disgusting and needs to be purged." Bethel's face had grown red with rage as he spoke.

"Purged?" Rhys asked calmly, refusing to stoop to his level of emotion. "What like we used to be? You know one theory on where that term comes from? It comes from what they would call the bundle of wood they used to burn us at the stake. That's one of the reasons why we hate that term. It has nothing to do with what we are or who we are, it's the term of how we were killed."

"Vermin sometimes need to burn."

That did it for Rhys. He had remained calm for most of the conversation, but Bethel was advocating extermination. He stood and grabbed Bethel by the lapels. "You little shit, you went after Sweet because he's smaller than you. You bastard! You put him in the hospital! Why didn't you come after me, hmm? Because you wouldn't stand a chance and you know it. You're a punk and a bully. You prey on those smaller than you so you can feel good about yourself."

"That's enough, Commander," his super ordered. Rhys turned fiery eyes to her.

"I'm tired of you protecting him, you daft cow. He may be your nephew, but he's a shitty person. If you can't see that, then so are you. You don't or refuse to see his flaws and you constantly cover for him. No more. This little shit needs to answer for his actions. I will be encouraging Sweet to file a lawsuit against him. And I will absolutely encourage him to include you and this department in that brief. Trust me, Collins' father is one of the best attorneys in London. He'll shut you down and make it so you and this little bitch of a nephew of yours will be slinging burgers for the rest of your miserable lives."

"Auntie!"

She dared not answer, opening her mouth and closing it like a fish. Rhys threw his elbow against Bethel's temple and let him drop. The weasel whimpered and curled into a ball.

"This department prides itself on diversity and inclusion but the second some homophobic racist little shit gets punched for spewing slurs and puts one of our own in the hospital, he comes running to Auntie to fix it. Sweet is ten times the man your nephew is and if you opened your eyes for one second you would know that. But it's all a lie to you, isn't it? Your team with a gay soldier as commander and a black gay man on the team is a token. It's all politics to you. It's all a game. These are our lives you're playing with. I wonder where he learned this behavior, *Auntie.*" Rhys pulled out his warrant card and tossed it on the table then opened the door of the office where several people had gathered to listen in. He smirked. "Oh, and by the way, most closeted gay men bully other gay men. Might wonder about

Bethel since I've caught him looking at *my* arse in the showers."

"That's – that's a lie!" Bethel sputtered but Rhys didn't listen... he wanted to get away. He needed to call Collins and Sweet but more importantly he wanted to call Kiter. He just needed to hear his voice.

After an hour on the phone with his brother, Kiter checked in with Boyd and Callum. They both claimed to be fine, but Kiter knew it was only a matter of time before they took matters into their own hands to avenge their fallen brothers. To make matters worse, HQ had received the funeral notices for three days form then. Kiter was going, even if his bosses told him not to. Search and rescue were able to retrieve the bodies of Darius and Hesler a day after they were killed and bring them home. He was not looking forward to facing the families again after giving them the news. He had tried to hold it together as he played the video for them and the parents and siblings cried when they announced they were married. According to some digging he had been able to do, they would be buried side by side, just like they did everything in life.

As he put away the dishes from his lunch, his phone rang. From the ringtone, he grinned and answered. "Miss me already?"

"You have no idea," Rhys replied and there was an edge to his voice that made Kiter take notice.

"What's wrong? What happened?"

"The bastard honestly said gays should be killed. Exterminated was the word he used."

"What?" Kiter breathed.

"Yeah, and guess what the super did?"

"What?"

"Nothing. She didn't do a damn thing. Her nephew, a member of her department calling for the eradication of an entire population and she sits there and tells me not to overreact."

"Oh hell no. What's this bitch's name?"

"What can you do? Can you do something? Anything?"

"Oh I can absolutely do something." The wheels in his head were already turning as to what he would be doing later that day before dinner. He'd have her badge before the sun set. "But enough about that. You're working for me now. And you know I won't advocate for that. You're safe. And I also wanted to see if Sweets and Collins would be interested."

"Really?"

"Well, you vouch for them. Sweets as you said is a master at accents, can blend in, we don't have anyone like that on our team. What's Collins expertise?"

"Sharpshooter."

"Even better."

"But he's not part of the LGBT community."

"You sure about that?" Kiter questioned.

Rhys paused for a moment. "Not on paper at least."

"I have another person in mind who isn't either. Not on paper at least. He's former SRR. Geoff's team." Kiter explained but Rhys went quiet, and he closed his eyes. *Dammit.* They were doing so well and he had to go and say the name of the one person who affected Rhys. "Rhys, I—"

"I know he's still in your life."

"Barely, I promise."

"No, no stop, I'm not upset. I... I think it's time we meet. Properly. With clothes *on* this time."

"Wait... really?" Kiter questioned.

"He's going to be in your life, and I want to be too so one time or another we will have to meet. I'd like it to be on my own terms."

"If you want to, but only if you do. You'd like Peter, his boyfriend. I think you two would get along."

"Just swear to me one thing, Sommerset," Rhys began.

"Anything."

"If you break this, that's it. No more chances, no more. You will be dead to me."

"I swear to you."

"Never cheat on me again."

"Never, I swear it. I'll even let you go through my phone everyday if you want just to prove it."

"I won't need to do that. I trust you at your word. But if you ever break this trust..."

"I won't."

Rhys took a breath. "I need to go to the hospital to check on Sweets. He should be discharged sometime today. Could we postpone our dinner and have the lads over? I think they need to hear what you have to offer. They won't want to be in that department any longer. They won't trust it."

"Yes, of course. Let's talk to them. I'd rather not go out and talk only because this is a top-secret group of guys."

"Come over to my place around 1900. I'll make lasagne."

"Can I help? I can bring a few things, or meet you at the market," Kiter offered.

Rhys paused. "Ehm, sure."

Kiter winced. "Too much?"

"No no, just processing. A lot's happened in a very short time, and I just need some time to process it all."

"Of course of course, I can be there at seven. Just tell me what you need. Can I bring anything?"

"How about some wine? Sweet likes sweet white and Collins like dry red."

"And you don't drink wine." Kiter said.

"You know me."

Kiter smiled. "Yes I do. You still like that boutique beer?"

"It's not boutique," Rhys laughed. "It's an American Pale."

"Like I said, boutique."

Rhys chuckled and Kiter could almost see him shake his head. "Be at my place at nineteen hundred, you can help me with some finishing touches."

"Right. I'll be there."

"And, Somm," Rhys stopped him from hanging up.

"Yeah?"

A pause, then, "thanks, for everything."

"My pleasure," Kiter ended the call and pocketed his phone. He had alcohol to pick up and. Maybe a dessert. A coffee cake, maybe? He chuckled and, grinning like a fool, he headed to the off license but sent an email to Marjorie saying to process the paperwork for Leo again when she got back into the office. They had a team to rally, and they had a traitor to find.

Chapter Eighteen

Rhys put the lasagna back in the oven and crumpled the aluminum foil he had wrapped around the edges. The cheese needed to brown. Turning the temperature down to allow it to brown slowly, he turned up the soft jazz music on his speakers. It was a quarter past and Kiter was late. He had sent a text letting him know he was almost there so Rhys didn't worry. Taking his whisky glass, he sat in the same recliner Kiter had sat in that night before.

Rhys shook his head, was that just the night before? It didn't seem possible. So much had happened in one day, Leo was still shocked he had kissed him, let alone played around in bed together. Being with Sommerset again was surreal and yet felt perfect. He had missed him. Had always loved him even when he was so damn angry at him but knowing he was about to knock on his door, share a space with him, speak to Sweet and

Collins about a new job opportunity, was everything he ever wanted.

He had just leaned his head back on the chair letting out a contented sigh when the expected knock sounded. His instant grin lit his face, and he pulled out of the chair heading to the door. Opening it, Kiter stood on the other side, a mirroring smile on his face.

"Sorry, I'm late. I didn't ruin anything did I?"

"Not at all, come in." Rhys stepped aside allowing Kiter to enter. Looking down at the three bags in his hands, Rhys chuckled. "Did you buy out the off license?"

Kiter shuffled. "Funny story," he began as he set the bags down on the kitchen island. "I wasn't sure what wine to get so I talked to one of the women who worked there and explained what I needed. She showed me bottle after bottle and confused the hell out of me with *tannis this* and *veritable grape that*, it was a disaster, so I had her pick her three favorites of each dry and sweet and it took her twenty minutes. Then, I wanted to find your American beer, but they didn't carry it. She looked it up and another store near St. Paul's had it, so I headed that way, but the computer was wrong. Fortunately, there were two others nearby. But neither of them stocked it either, so I bought you your Ardbeg Whisky hoping that would work. But as I was driving here, and traffic was a nightmare by the way, I passed one more just around the corner from you and thought, what the hell, why don't I go in to check and low and behold they had three cases, so I bought you two six packs and you have your whisky, and we have enough wine for three times as many people coming."

Rhys stepped up behind Kiter and wrapped his arms

around his waist, inching his hand up and across Kiter's chest. Kissing his shoulder, Rhys reveled in the fact Kiter stopped talking almost instantly, moaned, and leaned back against him. Kiter was only two inches shorter than Rhys and wrapped up together like that felt special.

"Hello, and thank you," Rhys whispered against his ear before nipping at his earlobe. His hands roamed Kiter's chest over his blue and white striped button up. Popping a few buttons, Rhys slipped his hands in and stroked Kiter's chest, feeling the coarse chest hair between his fingers. The man was always stunning, but the power he had coiled was what made Rhys weak.

Kiter turned his head and captured Rhys' lips with his, pressing his hand to the back of Rhys' head holding him close. Their kiss was sloppy given the angle, but Rhys loved every second. Hearing Kiter's gasps and moans as they plundered each other's mouths and bodies, made him want to say *screw dinner, come to bed.* But then Kiter turned in his arms, never breaking contact. He deepened the kiss as his hands slipped down Rhys' back to cup his ass through the stiff material of his jeans. Rhys groaned and ground himself against Kiter. Kiter let out a sexy grunt then backed them both up to the island. With the pressure on his lower ass, Rhys knew instinctively what Kiter wanted and with his help, he jumped up onto the counter far more gracefully than he expected and barely breaking their kiss. Kiter's hands were everywhere, and his scent filled Rhys' nose as his lips held his. Biting Kiter's lower lip, then soothing away the sting with his tongue, Rhys never wanted more than he did at that moment. Pulling back with the express purpose of telling Kiter to take him to the bedroom, he jumped when the timer for the oven went off.

"Shite!"

They panted, foreheads pressed together. Rhys' brain was foggy and as much as he was trying to think, his brain kept shouting *needneedneed* at him.

"I guess we got a bit carried away," Kiter teased.

"Aye," he answered. "I need... ehum... to... eh, check something."

Kiter grinned. "Always did think it was funny how you couldn't string a sentence together after a hot make out session."

Rhys gave him a sardonic look then his eyes went wide. "My lasagne!" He pushed Kiter out of the way and hopped down, his back twinging slightly. He grasped the counter and winced. Kiter held his arm, his eyes searching his face.

"Back," he replied motioning with his thumb and taking a deep breath.

"Let me get the food. Stay here." Kiter offered and Rhys, knowing he wouldn't be able to move at that moment, nodded. Kiter found the oven mitts and opened the door, pulling out the pan filled with his veggie lasagne. From the glimpse he got of it, it looked perfect. "Damn, this looks and smells amazing, babe," Kiter said setting it on the trivets Rhys had out. Rhys grinned through the stinging pain in his back hearing his man call him *babe*.

"Not bad, huh?" He teased and began to pull out the wine from the bags Kiter had brought. His hips were pressed against the island giving him support as his back continued to twinge.

"What can I do?" Kiter asked seeing the pain in his face.

"My Vicodin. It's in the bathroom medicine cabinet."

Kiter didn't hesitate, he hurried to the bathroom and came back with the prescription bottle. Pouring him a glass of water, he helped him with the lid and poured two pills into his hand. After he took the pain pills, Rhys allowed Kiter to pull one of the stools over and helped him sit in it.

"Damn back. It twinges like this all the time, but it'll go away soon."

"What else can I do?" Kiter asked.

"Could you get the salad bowl from the fridge and the cheese block? The Pecorino Romano will need to be grated over the lasagne and the salad."

"Sure," Kiter turned and opened the fridge pulling out the ingredients. "Grater?"

"Top drawer, left, island."

Kiter found it and began grating it over the top of the browned lasagne covering it in a fine dusting. Once the salad had its share of cheese, he set it down, washed his hands again, and got the wine opener.

"The woman said the red would need to air for a couple minutes. Might as well open it now."

Rhys nodded and slowly stood, his back beginning to feel better. "Wine glasses are here." He turned slowly and grabbed three glasses. Kiter moved around him in the kitchen flawlessly and it made Rhys happy. They fell back into their domestic routine so easily. They always cooked together. When they were dating, they used to entertain every month. Their friends and family coming over for dinner and games. Rhys would cook the main dish, but Kiter would help pull the meal together.

Just as Kiter poured the wine into the decanter Rhys had

forgotten he had in the back of a cabinet, there was a knock at the door. Busy melting the butter and adding garlic and Italian seasoning to a pan, Rhys looked over at him.

"Could you get that?" He asked.

Kiter finished pouring and nodded. Rhys watched him walk to the door to answer it as if they were an actual couple and Kiter lived with him. It still amazing him how quickly they had fallen back into their routine and how later, Rhys hoped they would... *enjoy* their new relationship. If Kiter touched him at all that night after his damn back spasmed. He'd just have to convince him, he was fine. After the pain pills kicked in, the muscles relaxed, and the bone didn't hurt as much. He would be fine. And he had waited eighteen years to have Kiter again. There was no way in hell he was going to allow them to just go to sleep.

Kiter couldn't wipe the lovesick look off his face as he crossed Rhys' living room to the front door. When Rhys' back twinged, Kiter worried he would be in too much pain, but once the meds kicked in, he was better. Moving in the kitchen, zigging to his zagging brought so many memories. His conversation with his brother earlier that day was still fresh in his mind. Jake was happy for him but warned him to be cautious of over doing it. He didn't want to scare Rhys away. Instead, he was ready to get down on one knee, but that would have to wait.

Opening the front door, he took in the two men standing before him. One was tall with heavy muscles like a wrestler, white with brown hair, and a closely trimmed beard. The other was only an inch or so shorter than him, well built, with sinewy muscles like a marathoner, black with kind eyes but the bruising around his face showed Kiter which was which.

"You must be Sweet and Collins," Kiter said sticking his hand out to them shaking both their hands.

"And you are?" Collins questioned.

"Come in lads, I'll explain everything," Rhys called from the kitchen.

Kiter stepped back and let them in noticing Sweet's slight limp and the way Collins hovered, never out of reach.

"Smells good in here, boss," Sweet said.

"None of that vegetarian, shite, right?" Collins asked.

Kiter was about to reply with a rebuke when Rhys threw his head back and laughed.

"Only you, Colins. You know that vegetarians make up twenty-two percent of the world's population *and* we have our origins back to ancient Egypt?" Rhys questioned.

"You know eating meat can trace it's origins back to cave men and tastes a whole hell of a lot better?" Collins grinned.

"Cave men, yes, and you omnivores still act like them. We've at least evolved into learned scholars and architects," Leo answered.

"Would you also consider marrying your sister to keep the bloodline pure, boss?" Collins tossed out.

Rhys laughed again as he pulled the garlic butter bread out of the oven. "Somm, could you pour the wine? Lads, this is Colonel Sommerset Kiter. Kiter, the lads."

"Kiter?" Sweet questioned.

"Yes," Kiter answered. "Good to meet you both."

Sweet's eyes passed from him over his shoulder toward Rhys, but Kiter wasn't quick enough to catch Rhys' look.

"What can I get you? We have a couple bottles of white and a red open and airing, apparently, according to the wine lady at the store," Kiter said.

"Red sounds good to me," Collins answered. "Like my wine like I like my food... bloody."

"Gross," Sweet replied, then turning to Kiter, he eyed him up and down, but not in a flirtatious way, more of a sizing him up sort of way. "What whites do you have, Colonel?"

"Please call me, Kiter," he said. "And I'll have you pick. They're all cold." After a moment of showing the wine bottles and getting immense satisfaction out of Sweet's reaction to one of the bottles, he poured three glasses of wine and grabbed Rhys' beer. The food was laid out on the kitchen island and as they got their plates to help themselves, Kiter had to consciously stop his thoughts from drifting to what he and Rhys had just done on that counter. A glance at Rhys showed he felt a bit better as he moved about the kitchen.

They were all talking about minor things like Collins' sons' game and how Sweet was feeling after being released from hospital. When they finally sat down at the table and began to eat, Kiter started to see why Rhys spoke so highly of them.

"So, what do you do, Colonel?" Collins asked him just as he took a bite of the best lasagne he had ever tasted. "Oops, sorry, take your time."

After Kiter swallowed, he spoke. "Please, it's Kiter or Sommerset, I'm not formal." He smiled. "I'm in intelligence."

"Like spy shit?" Sweet asked.

"Eh, kind of," Kiter answered.

"We actually wanted to talk to you lads together," Rhys began then turned to Sweet. "Nig, he's going to find out. Do you want to be the one to tell him?"

"Tell who what?" Collins asked. Kiter saw the look on Sweet's face and the soft resigned sigh he gave before turning to Collins.

"The man who attacked me. I do know who he is, but I didn't want to tell you."

"What?" Collins demanded. "Why didn't you tell me?"

"Because of this exact reaction and worse."

"Who the hell is it? I swear I will—"

"It was Bethel," Sweet answered like a bandaid ripping it off to help ease the pain.

Collins froze. "What?" His voice was low, and it nearly caused Kiter to shiver.

"Bethel cornered me in the locker room after you and Leo left. He said things. I threw the first punch. It was over after I was on the ground. He left and I crawled to the bench. I pulled myself up and waited there for a long time before being able to slip out unnoticed. I didn't tell you because I knew you would go all crazy and beat the ever-loving shit out of the man and I would lose you." Sweet bit his lip. "I mean the team would lose you. You're meant to be an officer, Gabe. If I had told you, you might have killed him, at best gotten suspended for attacking him. I'm not worth it."

"You are to me!" Collins shouted. The room went silent apart from Collins' panting. "We're partners, right? Best friends. You swore you would never lie to me."

Sweet reached for his hand. "And I didn't. That's why I didn't say anything. It wasn't a lie. I didn't lie to you. Leo figured it out. I told him when you went to get me some water. He understood why I couldn't tell you."

Collins stood and threw his napkin on the table.

"Where are you going?" Rhys asked.

"To find that son of a bitch and kill him."

"Gabe, please," Sweet begged. "Don't. Come back here. I need you with me. Please."

Collins was at the door by the time Sweet's plea reached his ears. He paused and took a deep breath.

"I know you're upset. I'm sorry," Sweet went on.

The scenario was too close for comfort for Kiter, and he stood, motioning with his hand for Sweet to wait a minute.

"Let's talk," he said to Collins and opened the front door. It shut slowly behind them as they stepped out into the hallway. "Look, I know how you must feel. If something happened to my partner, be it military, or personal I would want revenge. You care for Sweet. Love him even and never want to see him hurt. But what you're doing right now is hurting him. He needs you. He's scared for you. He's worried about his career. He needs the one person who is calm and his rock. That's you right now. I know you hate it. I know you want to go kill the son of a bitch, but that's not what Sweet needs right now. Take it from someone who wasted nearly twenty years of the best thing to ever happen to him. Go back inside, hear what Rhys and I have to say and be there for Nigel. He needs you."

"He should have told me."

"And there is probably a reason he didn't. You have kids, right?"

"Two boys."

"Is he close to them?"

"He's their godfather."

"Then that's probably why," Kiter said. "He was thinking

of your boys and how much they need you. How much he needs you. Can't you see how much he loves you?" Collins paled and Kiter quickly added. "Loves you as a brother, a best mate. He would never want you to be hurt because of him."

"But he's my best mate. I would kill anyone who hurt him."

"I know. I've been there. I get it. But for now, be calm and listen to him and us, yeah?"

After a second, Collins nodded.

"Good, lets get back in there," Kiter turned and knocked. Rhys opened the door and Kiter and Collins walked in. Collins went straight to Sweet and sat back down.

"Please understand why I didn't tell you," Sweet begged.

"I don't but I do."

"Oddly, I understood that. Please," Sweet took Collins' hand. "I need you here with me for now."

"I'm here, Sweets always." Collins' lip tipped up and he squeezed Sweet's hand. "So what happened, boss?"

"Well," Rhys began again after they all sat down. "I was summoned to the super's office."

"Am I relieved of duty?" Sweet asked.

"No, that is up to you. But... I am not your boss any longer," Rhys said.

"What are you talking about?" Collins asked after exchanging a glance with Sweet.

"I was called in to talk about what happened and lost my cool when Bethel was there and said some pretty terrible things. No," he held up his hand. "I will not repeat it. Just know I elbowed him to the temple, called the super a stuck-up bitch and left without my warrant card."

"Boss..." Collins began.

"That's got to be the hottest thing I've heard all day," Sweet beamed, then winced as the cut on his lip tugged.

"So I'm out as your boss, however, Somm and I have a plan. Somm?" He turned to him.

Kiter leaned forward. "I was vague about what I do earlier because I didn't want to jump the gun so to speak. I am MI6 and have been tasked with putting together an elite team. This team is sent in to places where MI6 wants and needs but cannot sanction. I will not lie to you; the last mission was a failure and I take full responsibility. We lost two good agents. But because of that, we are looking to replace them and to discover who was really behind the problems with the mission. Someone tipped off a very dangerous cartel and we lost not just our men but the mark as well. Whoever it was is a traitor to the UK and will be swiftly and severely punished. So, the reason I'm here is, Rhys has already accepted my job offer, he won't be team leader, but he will be second-in-command and he immediately thought of you two. Now, there is a catch. This team is supposed to be comprised of members of the LGBT community. Sweet, I know about you, but Collins, you're cis and straight from what I gather."

"He's an ally," Sweet defended.

"Still, on paper it would need to be something more."

"More like... what?" Collins asked.

"You would need to identify as one of the letters in the acronym," Kiter explained.

Collins leaned back. "And this paper I would be signing, would my boys ever find out? My wife?"

"No, it would be held in strict confidence." There was

silence around the table and Kiter continued. "I'm not asking for your answer now. Trust me I know how difficult it is to come out, as it were."

"You?" Collins asked.

"Yes, me," Kiter answered.

"In fact," Rhys took his hand. "Would this bother you?"

"Boss?" Sweet's eyes grew large.

"Yeah, we're back together."

"Back?" Collins questioned.

Then, Kiter went on. "You told him about me? You already knew. That's why you were studying me."

"Sorry, wanted to see what it was my friend saw in you. Now I do. But no, so long as you don't hurt him like you did before," Sweet said.

"That's water under the bridge, Sweet," Rhys replied.

"This is a lot to take in," Collins stated. "I've got my boys to think about. I can't say yes. There's a lot that goes into it. I can't... Amelie would kill me."

"I need you, Gabe. I don't want to do this on my own," Sweet pleaded.

Collins looked at him. "I've got the boys to consider, Nige. I can't say yes. But you can. Get away from that horrible man."

"You both can take some time," Kiter explained. "Contact Rhys when you've made your decision."

"Logistics, Kiter," Collins began. "Not to be crass but, what are we looking at in terms of compensation?"

"Twice your current annual salary plus housing allowance up to ten percent of your annual salary yearly. And for your boys, Collins," he went on. "If anything happened to you, their schooling will be paid for up to and including doctorate. They will get a yearly stipend of a quarter of your annual salary until they turn thirty years old. And Sweet for you, you'd name a beneficiary of your choosing to receive that same benefit. If, say the person you choose is over thirty, they will receive a lump sum of two and a half times your annual salary. Those are the terms of employment with the Charing Cross Boys."

"What if I choose Gabe's boys as my beneficiaries?" Sweet asked.

"Same rules apply. It's yours to name whoever you want."

Collins and Sweet glanced at each other. "Who is the team leader?"

"A man I trust with my life. He's a veteran of MI6. A spook by trade. Has countless successful missions under his belt," Kiter explained.

"He's impressive, I'll give him that," Rhys piped up.

Again Sweet and Collins were quiet, but Kiter watched as they communicated with each other wordlessly. Then, Sweet nodded once. "Okay. I'm in. With Rhys' recommendation, I'm in."

"Good," Kiter smiled at him, then turned to Collins. "I know how difficult this is. Take however long you need."

"Can you guarantee this team is open minded to Sweet's skin tone? I'm sick of people degrading him because of what he looks like. He's gorgeous and it is high time everyone sees it," Collins said. Everyone was silent.

"Thank you," Sweet finally said.

Collins didn't look at him as he kept his eyes on Kiter. He clearly realized what he said and was either embarrassed or fighting with himself. Kiter thought it might be both.

"I can guarantee the team will be open minded. Marks and upper management I cannot. But the good news is, you and Sweet will have very little interaction with them," Kiter promised.

"That's something at least." Collins was quiet for a long moment. "I wouldn't be the cop I am today without Leo and Sweets. I couldn't imagine going in in the morning without them there. I... I can identify as Questioning. That's on the scale, right?"

"Yeah," Sweet said. "Are you sure? There are other, safer options."

"Like?" Collins finally looked at him.

"Demi-sexual, pansexual, aromantic, just to name a couple."

"I have no idea what those mean."

"I don't want you to claim something and regret it later," Sweet said.

Collins stared at him. "And if I'm not claiming it, and truly feel that way?"

Sweet swallowed hard. "That would be... different."

"Then don't question what I'm claiming," he said. "It's difficult enough to finally admit it to someone other than myself."

Sweet bit his lower lip and Kiter noticed how Collins' eyes dropped to that movement.

"Well... I'm happy to have you both on board. I'll have our team's admin Marjorie start the transfer paperwork," Kiter said. "Glad to have you both on the CCB team."

The two weren't paying any attention to him as they kept staring at each other.

"Dessert?" Rhys finally said loud enough they jumped and looked away from each other sheepishly.

"Sounds good, boss... I guess I'll have to get used to calling you Campbell?" Collins shuddered.

"God no," Rhys said. "It's Leo before it's ever Campbell."

"Leo... I can get with that," Collins answered.

Rhys stood and headed to the kitchen. Kiter followed closely behind him.

"That went better than I expected," Rhys whispered.

"Yeah, if those two don't end up together, I'm cancelling my subscription to romances anonymous."

Rhys laughed. "That was unexpected, I'll admit. Still, good to know you have a romantic streak."

"Oh yeah? Why?"

"I'm not just any girl you get to take to bed, Colonel. This arse needs some romance," Rhys pecked a quick kiss on Kiter's lips.

"Just wait until they leave and see how romantic I can be," Kiter said.

"Lads," Rhys called and turned with the coffee cake Kiter had picked up. "It's a slice and you're out of here."

Sweet chuckled while Collins looked clueless. "Oh for feck's sake, Gabe," Rhys sighed exasperated. "Do I have to spell it out?"

"Oh... Oh! God, no, thanks for that image, boss. Ehum..."

"Oh my poor little straight baby," Sweet said. "Whatever are we going to do with you?"

"I'm sure you'll come up with something," Rhys teased.

The door closed behind Sweet and Collins and Rhys breathed out. Everything was going as planned and as Rhys turned back to the kitchen, he saw his man leaning up against the kitchen island. All the dishes had been washed and were on the drying rack and the kitchen was clean. Kiter's hand caressed the countertop where Rhys had sat not three hours before. Rhys flushed remembering the needy sounds he had made but his heart swelled when he remembered how tender Kiter was when he had twisted his back. He grinned when he saw Kiter holding two tumblers of the Ardbeg Scotch he had bought him.

"Nightcap?" Kiter asked.

"Love one," Rhys replied sauntering over to him and taking the glass he offered. There wasn't much in there as Rhys had already had two beers and two Vicodin earlier, but it smelled peaty and divine. It was his favorite and something in his chest expanded with joy knowing Kiter had remembered.

"What do we drink to?" Rhys asked.

"Life? The future? Each other? Together?" Kiter offered.

"Sounds like you have a lot to toast to."

"Thanks to the most amazing man giving me a second chance."

"He sounds pretty incredible," Rhys grinned.

"He's humble too," Kiter teased.

"Of course. The humblest," Rhys winked and waited.

"To those who have passed on but taught us so much about how to live each day like it was our last. To the men who came before us to pave the way so we can be here together with no concern nor regret. And to each other outgrowing our past for a shot at a bright future one I will never take for granted." Kiter clinked his glass to Rhys', and they drank. The burn of the alcohol was familiar but the burning in his eyes as he watched Kiter was new. Something was on his mind. Setting the glass down on the counter, Rhys took Kiter's hand.

"Talk to me. What's going on? You seem sad."

Kiter breathed out. "I received the funeral notification for Darius and Hesler. It's Friday."

"You have to go."

"I know. But I don't want to go alone."

Rhys took Kiter's glass and set it beside his, then cupped his face in his hands. "You will never be alone again, my love. Not as long as there is breath in my lungs and blood pumping in my heart. I am here. I am yours. And I will never let you be alone again." A single tear fell from Kiter's eye and Rhys wiped it away. "Come to bed with me, my love. Be with me. Make love to me."

"I love you, Rhys Campbell. I always have and I always will."

"Then that is all that matters tonight." With that, Rhys took his hand and led him into the bedroom.

Chapter Nineteen

Two Months Later

Rhys leaned back in the chair in the lecture hall of the Charing Cross Boys' offices rocking back and forth listening to Kiter's presentation. His left hand rested on his upper thigh and his right was holding his pen to the small pad of paper. Kiter was giving the brief on their next op but Rhys could barely concentrate. His man looked damn good up there, commanding the room. It had been two months since Sweet and Collins had joined the CCBoys and as he looked around the room, tearing his gaze off Kiter's strong chest encased in a white button up shirt, he saw the two of them sitting side by side listening. Boyd and Callum sat behind him and after an initial awkwardness between Boyd and Rhys, they put their past behind them and he deemed him a friend. Since then, Boyd had attached himself to Rhys like a mentor and though it was odd given their intimate history, Rhys looked at him like a kid brother and they grew close. The entire team was close, apart from Callum. Callum was more difficult to read, and Rhys respected that. As Team Leader, Callum needed to maintain a sort of aloofness. He never made his team feel inferior, but he never revealed much about himself.

Rhys' eyes fell back on Kiter as he pushed up the sleeves on his shirt revealing his strong forearms. Rhys sank his teeth into his lower lip to bite back a groan of appreciation when Kiter locked eyes with him.

"Leo," he said. "What are your thoughts?"

"Sorry? Thoughts on what?"

Kiter gave him a disapproving teacher look that Rhys found endearing.

"I asked what your thoughts were on this project since you have the experience with this group of anarchists," Kiter stated.

"I'll be honest, I wasn't paying attention."

Kiter growled.

"What? It's not my fault! It's yours. You look ridiculously hot up there. All commanding and shite. If you want me to actually pay attention, you should have Callum do the briefing."

"Gee, thanks for telling me I'm not hot," Callum teased from behind him.

Rhys shrugged. "You're welcome."

"Leo, pay attention," Kiter ordered.

"Yes, Daddy," Rhys grinned. Boyd and Sweets squealed in delight while Callum and Gabe chuckled.

"Don't make me take you over my knee," Kiter replied.

"Promises promises," Rhys winked. He heard the laughter and felt Boyd patting his back as if saying good job. But it was Kiter's reaction he watched. His man gave a long-suffering sigh and shook his head.

They had played around with kinks in the bedroom over the last few weeks, and Rhys could honestly say the Daddy/boy dynamic was not for him. But he thoroughly enjoyed the spankings. Kiter allowed the teasing and chatter between the teammates for a few moments, before calling their attention back to the matter. That was one thing Rhys loved about the team. They had to be serious, of course, it was life and death but there were times when they were allowed to just be men, friends, tease each other respectfully, and enjoy being part of such a diverse group. Kiter's motto was always *what was life without a little fun thrown in?* And Rhys couldn't agree more.

"All right, all right, settle down," Kiter called. "Leo... I'll see you after class," he winked. Rhys' grin bloomed seeing the promise in his eyes.

Once everyone was back to focusing on the mission, Kiter finished the briefing. It was an extraction job. A head of state for one of the countries in the EU was accused of perpetrating horrific crimes against British nationals abroad. Kidnapping, rape, extortion, murder, it didn't matter so long as his pockets were lined. He liked them exotic and focused his attention on members of British territories such as the Caribbean Islands, the Iberian Peninsula, and the outlying Atlantic Ocean and Indian Ocean islands. He was discovered to be in London on business and was followed by another MI6 team until the members of that team were found dead in their car. Marjorie had found one of the man's aliases had purchased passage on the Chunnel Train and it was up to CCB to stop him before he crossed into French territory.

It was also known the man had no preference for either men or women as he enjoyed both so they would use his known attraction against him. Collins would play patsy and flirt, getting him alone somehow and give him a paralytic. Sweet and Rhys would take care of his bodyguards while Boyd and Callum would hack into the security system and shut down the power if they got too close to the border. They needed a good escape plan and that was where Kiter came in. He would be in the HQ van inside the service maintenance tunnel watching everything on his monitors. Once they had their target, they would administer the antidote so the paralysis didn't become permanent and leave through a maintenance hatch where Kiter would meet them with a vehicle. With luck it would go off without a hitch. But Rhys knew how worried Kiter was. It was the first big mission the team had been on since they had lost Hesler and Darius.

Whatever Rhys could do to calm his nerves, he would. Kiter needed to keep his head in the game. They had the mission. He had their backs.

"You think you're terribly clever, don't you?" Kiter questioned not looking up as he clicked out of the short presentation once they were alone.

"Don't know what you mean. I've never been bad in my life," Rhys teased.

Kiter barked a laugh, then looked up at him. Crooking his finger, he beckoned him to the front of the room. Rhys stood and hurried down to him. The briefing room, unlike the boardroom was set up like a lecture hall, complete with platform for presentations and desks chairs. As Rhys hopped up on the stage to be face to face with his lover and best friend, he waited. Kiter stared at him for a long moment.

"What am I going to do with you?" He asked.

"I have a few ideas," Rhys bounced his eyebrows suggestively.

"Disrupting class, snarky feedback, disrespectful behavior... I think someone needs to be spanked."

Rhys' blood pounded through his veins and heated him from head to toe with excitement. "That doesn't sound like a punishment."

Kiter stroked his knuckles down Leo's jaw and leaned in just enough to feel his breath on his lips but not enough to kiss him.

"Turn around."

Leo's breath came in short pants as he turned his back. Kiter's hand pressed at the base of his spine and slowly slid upwards, goosebumps ran up and down Leo's arms and legs as he anticipated Kiter's next move. Sure enough, there was a pressure at the back of Leo's neck pushing him down. Leo folded himself over the table before him. As his shirt-covered chest met the cool desk, he let out a sigh of relief. The cool touch eased his skin.

Kiter's hand slipped back down from the back of Leo's head following the same path as before, sending more goosebumps up and down Rhys' body. Soon Kiter's hand stopped just at the top curve of Leo's ass. And vanished. Leo's breathing picked up as he waited. But after twenty seconds, nothing had happened, and Rhys squirmed. That was when he felt the first strike of Kiter's palm. The jolt had him crying out and his pants tightening over his groin.

Kiter's hand soothed the sting and Leo grew restless

again. After fifteen seconds, the hard smack happened again, and Leo whimpered as a wet spot began to grow on his boxers. Kiter could turn him on with merely a look and make him a puddle of precum in seconds.

"Do you know why you're being punished?" Kiter's voice was strained as if he was holding back his arousal.

"Yes, sir," Rhys answered.

Another smack.

"Tell me why."

"Because I wasn't paying attention."

Another smack.

"And?"

Rhys' mouth was dry. "And because I disrupted the class by calling you Daddy."

Another smack and Rhys groaned. It was his favorite roleplay.

"And why don't I want you to do that?" Kiter asked.

"Because our sex life is ours."

"And no one else's." Kiter finished with another smack and smoothed his hand over Leo's burning ass.

"Please, I'm sorry. Please."

"What do you want, Rhys?" Kiter's voice was low and heavy.

"I want... I want..."

"Tell me."

"You. I want you, baby."

"Good," Kiter said. There was a shuffle of clothes as he leaned over him and popped the button of Rhys' jeans and slid the zipper down. Cool air hit the overheated skin of his ass. "Such a pretty color." Kiter caressed Leo's cheeks.

"Please," Leo begged.

"Patience."

"No."

Kiter drew his hand away and Leo groaned. The palm of Kiter's hand landed with a loud smack on Leo's right cheek. Rhys cried out as the sting morphed into pleasure.

"I'm in control," Kiter stated. "Understand?"

"Yes, yes, I'm sorry. Just please."

Kiter soothed his palm down the part of him that was on fire. Rhys closed his eyes and listened. He whimpered when he heard the telltale sound of foil tearing. He let out a sigh of relief as Kiter's fingers found his hole and slid in. The burn was magical. But when he added a second, then a third Rhys thought he might come right then. He was harder than he'd ever been in his life.

Finally, Kiter removed his fingers and Rhys nearly cried out in frustration but was silenced by Kiter's single hard thrust. He was buried to the hilt and Rhys let out a cry at the sudden burning, but it soon morphed into pleasure. Kiter's hand caressed his side, but he didn't move, allowing him to adjust to his girth. Rhys reached behind him, grasping at Kiter's hip. Kiter pulled out nearly all the way, then slammed back in. Rhys let out a cry as Kiter hit that spot inside him. Again and again Kiter pulled out slowly, only to slam back inside. He was aching with need, dripping with precum.

"Somm, Somm, please."

"You like that? You did it deliberately, didn't you? You wanted your punishment."

"I wanted you," he groaned as Kiter brushed over his prostate again. The pressure at the base of his spine began to build. "Somm, I'm close," he warned.

"Me too. Come for me, Rhys," Kiter breathed, and Rhys let go. Wave after wave crashed over him as he let out a cry. He felt Kiter speed up, swell inside him, and grunt. The feeling of his lover spilling inside him, of knowing he caused him pleasure, was too much and another wave crashed over him.

When he finally came to his senses, he felt Kiter's lips on his shoulder. He moved his head, heavy after such an intense orgasm and captured Kiter's lips. They kissed lazily until Kiter slipped gently out of him. Still, he moaned feeling the effects of such a rough coupling. But Kiter never stopped kissing him.

"I love you, baby," he said softly.

"I love you too, Somm," Rhys panted.

"And you can call me Daddy anytime. Just always pay attention. I can't lose you on a mission, all right?"

Rhys nodded and turned to face him. "Aye, I will. But you won't lose me, Somm."

"I could and it would destroy me."

"Me too," Rhys cupped his face. "But you must know I'm a professional. I know what I'm doing, and we won't be entrenched like that again. I know you still worry after what happened, but baby, trust me when I say, you will have me for a very long time by your side."

"I want that."

"Me too. But for the record, I don't think the best way is through the train station, I think we need to already be in the tunnel. Boyd said he can hack the system to slow the train down enough to allow us to get on. If we stop it altogether, he might get suspicious. Oh, and I don't think Collins is the right one to capture the mark. The man loves exotic. Collins, though handsome, isn't exotic enough. He and Sweet need to switch places. Besides, Sweet can seduce another man. Collins is straight. I also think Sweet should put on one of his Caribbean accents. I also think I should take Callum's place with Boyd. Callum will be needed with Collins to subdue the guards."

Kiter paused, their eyes locked. "You... think Collins is handsome?"

Rhys rolled his eyes. "Wow, out of all of that, that was what you got?"

Kiter gripped Rhys' ass. "Everything else makes sense. I knew you were paying attention."

"No, you didn't," Rhys chuckled.

Kiter kissed him softly and pressed his forehead to his. "Solid plan, Rhys. I'll have Marjorie make the necessary changes. Promise me you'll be okay. That you'll watch out and take care of yourself. I can't lose you."

"You won't," Rhys placed a quick peck on his nose. "I'll be fine. Promise."

Chapter Twenty

All was not fine. Kiter watched the team as they reached the train Boyd had gotten to slow down enough to board. But the door was sticking. The computer was faulty and couldn't open the luggage car door. Their window of opportunity was shrinking fast.

"Autolycus, status," Kiter demanded.

"Worthless piece of shit," Boyd berated the computer. "We need to have a serious talk about technology."

"Just blow it," Callum said and nodded at Gabe who moved into position and shot the handle off the door. The luggage car door slid open with a bang.

"Thank you!" Boyd shouted.

"Easy," Rhys placed a hand on Boyd's shoulder calming him.

Collins was first in and swept the car with his M4.

"Clear." He called and everyone else jumped up into the car. Callum tugged the door shut.

"Scorpio, We're in," Callum spoke calmly over the comms.

"Good, get the target and get out," Kiter ordered.

"Tracking shows Kyetti's in First Class," Boyd said. "Time needs to move up by five minutes."

"Affirmative, moving timetable up by five," Kiter said. Everyone fixed the times on their watches.

"Diamond, you're up," Callum called to Sweet. Diamond was his codename because at University and early in his police career, everyone used to sing *Sweet Caroline* around him all the time, Neil Diamond's song. And since his first name was Nigel, close enough in some of their minds, *Diamond* stuck.

Sweet pulled up his briefcase and set it on one of the other suitcases. Popping the top, he striped out of his tactical gear and pulled on a button up shirt, and black dress slacks. Collins stood nearby ready to help. Striping to his black briefs Sweet hurriedly changed clothes. He took Collins' arm when offered to pull on his shoes. Once he was dressed, he nodded once at Callum and Collins and pulled out the nerve agent from the briefcase. Coating his hand in the oil, he had five minutes before it activated. Enough time to find the mark, talk, and shake hands, transferring the nerve agent to Kyetti. Once done, Sweet nonchalantly walked toward the door.

"Be careful," Collins called to him.

Sweet turned and gave a small smirk. "Always am."

"Scorpio, Diamond is delivering the package," Callum spoke into comms.

Kiter switched to Sweet's camera, watching as he made

his way to the first-class car.

"Target acquired," Sweet said low as his eyes caught the man seated in the window seat. Four goons surrounded him.

"It's a go, Diamond," Kiter said.

Without answering, Sweet fell into the seat across the aisle facing the other way. He looked over seeing the glass of champagne in front of their target.

"Excuse me," he said in a Caribbean Island accent. The man looked over, his brow raising slightly as he eyed Sweet. One of the goons took a step closer. "Oh, Jesus, sorry. I was just goin' to ask what you're drinkin'. It looked good. Din't mean to bother ya."

Sweet leaned away from him and pulled out his phone. The man made a tsking noise aimed at the body guard and then spoke to Sweet.

"Sorry about him. They're overcautious. This is Louis Roederer Cristal, twenty years old."

"Oh, I'm guessing it's expensive. I'm a cheap brut kinda guy."

"Ah," then he leaned further toward him. "Forgive me, but do I detect a British Virgin Island's accent?"

"Yep, born and raised. I'm surprised you can hear the difference. Most people just say Jamaican or Caribbean Islander."

"I'm not most people. Most people are idiots. An accent can tell a lot about a man," Kyetti said.

"Oh? And what does mine say?"

"That you're fun," he answered.

Sweet grinned. "I can be. My ex wouldn't agree though."

"Oh no?"

"No, he was a stick in the mud," Sweet laughed. The attendant came over to him.

"Can I get you something to drink, sir?" She asked.

"He'll have some of mine. Bring another glass," Kyetti said.

"Oh I couldn't possibly."

"I insist. Don't let it be said anyone near me has some cheap champagne."

"Well, thank you, that's kind of you." Sweet smiled at him and the attendant left to get the glass.

"I didn't see you on the train earlier."

"Nervous traveller," he said. "I stayed in the cabin my company got for me. But I needed a drink."

Kyetti nodded slowly and then offered the seat opposite him. Sweet moved to sit down.

"Hook's in," Kiter stated. "Two minutes, Diamond." With that announcement, Rhys and Boyd opened the door and headed in the opposite direction toward the control center. Kiter listened to the rest of Sweet's conversation as he and the target shared the champagne.

"All I'm saying is don't date someone who has no taste for champagne," Sweet said. "Especially this, it's delicious."

"I'm glad you like it, my friend," the target said. "Forgive me, I didn't ask your name."

"Jethro Taylor." Sweet offered his hand and the target shook.

"Nerve agent dispersed," Kiter said over comms as Sweet shook hands.

"Major Kyetti."

"Italian?" He wasn't but the last name sounded Italian

enough that Sweet was able to play it off. "Baby, my luck is getting better and better."

"Blue team, status?" Kiter asked.

Leo answered. "Breaching command in three... two... one." There was no noise as Leo and Boyd entered the command control room. The pilot held up his hands. "We're not going to hurt you," Leo assured. "But we need you to slow the train down. Now."

The pilot did as they asked, and the train slowed abruptly. Kiter looked back at Sweet's camera to see all the passengers in that car cry out in exclamation at the sudden jerk. Sweet conveniently jerked and splashed champagne over his hand with the nerve agent, effectively wiping it off and then he reached into the briefcase for the antidote wrapped in paper napkins. He wiped his shirt and pants. The needle piercing the skin of his thigh as he pretended to wipe it off giving himself the antidote.

"Damn, what a waste," he clicked his tongue.

The target spoke to two of his goons. "Go, find out what happened." They left and Kyetti looked back at Sweet. "Are you all right, my friend?" He asked.

"Yes, thanks, sorry. I didn't mean to spill it. I'm all wet."

"It happens, no harm done."

"What do you think happened?" Sweet asked.

"My men are going to find out."

"Sorry, but men? I mean, baby, if I had a bunch of hot guys around me, I'd never let them leave my side."

"They're not for pleasure, believe me."

"Oh... they're like..." Sweet looked around before lowering his voice. "Bodyguards?"

Kyetti smirked. "I'm a very dangerous man."

"No, you? I don't believe it." Sweet leaned back and stared. "Well... maybe I could see you being a bit naughty, but not dangerous."

"Can you be?"

"Be what?"

"Naughty."

"Oh baby, like you would never believe," Sweet said.

"Prove it."

Sweet stared at him and Kiter counted the seconds before the nerve agent took over. They had about three minutes. After a beat, Sweet continued. "Sorry, 'scuse me, miss?" He called to one of the attendants. She looked over. "Where's the bathroom?"

"Down the hall," she answered.

Kiter watched as a salacious grin spread across Kyetti's face. Sweet offered a hand to the older man. "Want to find out how naughty I can be?" Sweet asked.

"Oh with pleasure."

"Sir," one of the bodyguards began. "We haven't assessed the situation yet. I would prefer you to stay within my line of sight."

"And I would prefer you not question me. We'll be within earshot of you and the train is not moving. How much danger can I be in?" With that Sweet and Kyetti moved down the car to the next room, the security guard behind him. As soon as Sweet opened the door, the guard pushed him out of the way and did a quick perimeter check.

"I mean if you wanna get down like that, I'm game," Sweet said.

The guard grunted and stepped back. "When I get back," Kyetti started speaking to the guard. "We're going to have a serious discussion about your behavior."

"Diamond, two minutes," Kiter warned.

Sweet gave the motion they had set to say understood, clenching his fist as if cracking or stretching their fingers. Kyetti then entered the bathroom, which was oddly spacious and Sweet slowly shut the door. Once they were alone, Sweet pushed Kyetti against the door. The man gave a pleased grunt and grinned. Sweet moved in and unbuttoned Kyetti's collar buttons, kissing his way along his neck, biting and sucking. The camera was worthless as Sweet's lapel was flush with Kyetti's and covered the camera but there were unmistakable grunts and pants as he continued kissing him for a good thirty seconds.

"Off," Kyetti panted. "I want to see you."

"With pleasure," Sweet said and pulled back enough to pull off his suit jacket and unbutton his shirt but never removing it fully as that was where his body camera was.

"Reaper, focus," Kiter heard Callum say to Collins.

Looking over at Callum's camera and saw Collin's obviously listening to the sounds and getting more and more angry.

"Reaper, not now," Kiter said.

Unable to worry about Collins' reaction, he looked at the clock just as he watched Sweet go to his knees in front of Kyetti and took his belt off with a flourish. "Incapacitate in three... two... one." Kiter ordered.

With belt in hand, Sweet stood and turned Kyetti around forcefully taking his hands behind him and slipping the belt around his wrists tightening. Kyetti grunted.

"No touchy, daddy," Sweet said.

"Time," Kiter replied.

Turning Kyetti around, the camera caught his slightly stoned look as the nerve agent took hold. "Agent Diamond, Mr. Kyetti of Her Majesty's Secret Service. You, sir, are under arrest for crimes against Britain," Sweet said.

Kyetti tried to call out but couldn't. The paralytic froze his vocal cords first. Holding on to him, Sweet knocked on the door twice and Collins and Callum opened it.

"Well done," Callum replied.

"You all right?" Collins questioned quickly.

"Fine," Sweet confirmed. Then his eyes went down to the two prone bodies on the floor. "You good?"

"Nothing I couldn't handle," Collins replied.

Callum reached in for Kyetti who weakly tried to wave him off. "Come with us, Mr. Kyetti. We have a holding cell with your name on it." Callum got him up and he and Collins carried him back to the luggage car where Rhys and Boyd waited.

"Package in hand, Scorpio," Callum confirmed.

"Escape inbound," Kiter said. Then, glancing at the drone footage showing the incoming vehicle, Kiter heard the ruckus and a gunshot. His stomach pitched and his eyes darkened as he took two second to look back at the camera screen of his team.

"Leo!" Callum shouted and Kiter's world went black.

Then, he ran.

Chapter Twenty-One

Rhys didn't trust the target. Kyetti was a slippery fish with four failed attempts at capture. He kept his eyes on him as Callum administered the antidote so he could move when they needed him to. But something didn't sit right with him. So Rhys watched, his finger not too far from the trigger of his military grade weapon.

"Package in hand, Scorpio," Callum said over comms.

"Escape inbound," Kiter replied, and Boyd opened the door to look out. The train was barely moving.

"I see it," Boyd called and then looked down at his little computer screen as if guiding the drone to their location. But just as Boyd looked up as the drone hovered overhead, Rhys saw the movement. Kyetti lunged forward and grabbed one of the guns on Collins' belt and aimed it at Boyd. Rhys stepped in front and raised his gun at the same time Kyetti fired. Rhys felt the punch in his chest just as he fired hitting Kyetti in the arm.

"Leo!" Callum shouted. But the world was inverting and going black.

"Rhys, Rhys, baby, come on, open your eyes. Please, I need you."

Somm, Somm needed him. Rhys needed to open his eyes, but he couldn't get his breath back.

"The vest caught it, boss," another voice. He knew that voice, but he couldn't place it.

"He's gonna be hurtin' tomorrow." Collins, that was Collins.

"Rhys, come on, baby, please."

Leo grunted. He couldn't catch his breath, but he had to reassure Kiter. He was okay. But the pain in his chest radiated. He paused gaining the strength he needed, then he slowly opened his eyes. Somm leaned over him. The first thing he saw was his face filled with worry.

"Shite, I got shot," Leo grunted.

There were chuckles from others around him apart from Kiter who closed his eyes for a brief moment then helped him sit up.

"Never do that to me again, understand?" Kiter whispered in his ear as he helped him sit up. Rhys kissed him quickly then nodded.

"Not my first choice," he grunted.

Kiter pressed his forehead to Rhys'. "I love you."

"Love you too."

"Come on, let's get you up," Kiter helped him stand and Rhys held in his grunt as the pain radiated down his torso.

"Where's Kyetti?" Rhys questioned.

"Over there," Callum said indicating the man bound and gagged behind a large piece of luggage. The bullet wound in his arm caused blood to trickle down and drip to the floor.

"Can you walk?" Kiter asked.

"Aye, I'm good, just got the wind knocked out of me," Rhys said.

"Let's get you out of here," Kiter replied.

Rhys then felt the stillness of the train. He looked around and Boyd held up his device. "Scorpio's orders. Keep the train stopped so he could get on. Never seen a man run that fast."

"Everyone all right?" Marjorie's voice came over the comms from where she had stayed in the maintenance tunnel with all the screens when Kiter ran out.

"Aye, we're good, Mama Bear." Kiter called to her.

"Good, you got incoming, you gotta move."

"Time to go," Callum stated as he and Collins dragged Kyetti to his feet and tossed him out of the car allowing him to land hard on the floor. "Oops, Reaper, you shouldn't have shoved me."

"Sorry, Frax," Collins answered playing along. "Let's get him up." They hopped down from the luggage car and picked Kyetti up then Collins punched him in the stomach as Callum held him up. "Man, you're just all over the place right now. Must be that paralytic." They dropped him again.

"Oh, Kyetti, you fell down, here let me help you up," Callum said as he pulled the man up

"Enough play," Kiter call holding Rhys' arm as he walked gingerly to the edge of the luggage car. "I get it, but let's get going."

Sweet hopped down and walked over to Collins who

slung his arm around him. "Good job, Diamond."

"Thank you, thank you, I'll be ready to pick up my Academy Award tonight."

They laughed and piled into the car. Kiter helped Rhys down from the luggage car and held him close for a moment.

"You scared me," Kiter said.

"I'm sorry," Rhys answered. "But aren't you glad I decided to wear this?" He indicated his Kevlar vest.

"You're never doing another mission without it." Rhys smiled as Kiter cupped his face. "I'm going to take you home."

"I like that plan. I'm tired."

"I wonder why?" Kiter asked sarcastically. "But I have to stop in at the office."

"What? Why?"

"Our newest member of the team is coming in tomorrow and I have to sign a couple things."

"Newest... oh right..." Rhys smirked. "Have you told the boys?"

"Not yet," Kiter replied. "I want it to be a surprise."

"You like springing things on people, huh?"

"Sometimes."

"Scorpio, Leo, come on! Let's get a move on. You two can make kissy face later."

Kiter chuckled but didn't look back. "I swear, I could kill Callum sometimes."

"You love him like a son, don't give me that," Rhys said.

"Son? Please, do I look old enough to have a brat that age?"

"Ehum... not sure how to answer that," Rhys winked.

"You're one rude arsehole, you know that?" Kiter teased.

"You have to be nice to me," Rhys stated. "I just got shot."

"How long are you going to be milking that?"

"As long as I can."

"I bet you are," Kiter kissed him quickly then turned to the team who were making *ooh* sounds as if they were teenagers. "I swear, I run a team of children. Children, I tell you."

"And that team of children just saved England." Collins said.

"Yeah we did!" Boyd cheered.

"And had fun doing it," Sweet answered.

"Autolycus, what do you say we let the rest of these people go? Put the train back in service," Kiter said sliding in beside Rhys.

"Sounds good," Boyd clicked a few places on his tablet and soon the train began moving again.

"Let's get home, boys," Kiter replied putting the car in gear and slipping into the emergency maintenance hatch and driving away just before the boys in blue showed up.

"Scorpio," Marjorie called over the comms.

"Go for Scorpio," Kiter said.

"New recruit is confirmed for tomorrow. I'm heading to HQ to get paperwork."

"Sounds good, Mama Bear," he replied. "I'll meet you there."

"New recruit?" Boyd asked.

"Another teammate?" Collins questioned.

"That makes seven." Rhys replied.

"Six," Kiter answered. "I'm not going to be in the field much. I was filling in. I'll be calling shots at HQ, behind the scenes."

"Who is it, boss? Anyone we know?" Sweet asked.

"Don't think so," Kiter answered. "Boyd'll know him."

"I will?" Boyd asked.

"You will," Kiter confirmed. "How are you feeling?"

"Just a little bruised. Why?" Rhys asked.

"Beer?"

"Oh dear god yes," he replied.

"Good," he kissed his temple. "Let's drop this bastard off and go to the pub, boys."

The team cheered and Callum spoke teasingly. "One mission down, boys. Only nine hundred seventy-nine to go."

They chuckled but Boyd grew serious. "And one to avenge."

Kiter and Rhys exchanged a look. "Remember, we are not hired guns. We are Her Majesty's Secret Service. Whatever we do reflects on the monarchy." Kiter warned.

"You don't want to know who betrayed us, boss?" Callum questioned.

"I didn't say that," Kiter replied. "I want to find them more than you know. But let's go about this the right way."

"Or we could set the world on fire and watch it burn," Rhys said.

"Spoken like a true Leo," Kiter teased.

"Don't rain on my parade, Scorpio," Rhys chuckled.

After a moment, they exited the tunnel and the bright sunlight shown down on them. "Beautiful day." Kiter breathed deeply.

"We're going to find the traitor, boys. That's a promise."

"We got this. Let's roll," Kiter replied.

To Be Continued in Book Two:

Sweet Caroline

Acknowledgements

Thank you all so much for reading! I hope you enjoyed Kiter's and Rhys' story!

I have loved Sommerset Kiter since the beginning of Geoff and Peter's story; Take My Breath Away. When I wrote about a Scotsman named Leo in *Love Among the Shamrocks Collection, The Next Generation The Song of Heart's Desire*, I was intrigued. I always thought I would write Kiter's story but to have Leo make an appearance was fascinating. *The Charing Cross Boys* have their origins in *Love Among the Shamrocks Collection, The Next Generation You Don't Own Me*. Which will be Callum's and Killian's story and was written first but as soon as I wrote the characters, I knew they had some sort of history and thus this series began.

If you are interested in some of the external aspects of this book, please take a look at the series *Love Among the Shamrocks Collection, The Next Generation* and *Love Among the Shamrocks Universe Take My Breath Away* is Peter and Geoff's story and parts of it takes place during this time. You get to meet the SSR team and learn more about Geoff's relationship with his father, the homophobic Duke.

I wanted to thank my cousin, Alex, for his military expertise in helping me make the military parts as accurate as I could. Thank you for your service. I love you, brother! Stay safe! I also wanted to thank my beta readers for their contribution and support. This was their second MM book and I think they thoroughly enjoyed it.

I also have to say thank you to my parents for their love and support during this very difficult time. You mean so much to me and I couldn't imagine going through this tough time without you!

I hope you loved Rhys and Sommerset as much as I did! Please consider leaving a review on your favorite site and don't forget to follow me on social media under the handle M. Katherine Clark Author! And be sure to sign up for my newsletter at www.mkatherineclark.net! Keep an eye out for my next release; Book Two of the series; *The Charing Cross Boys: Sweet Caroline.*

THE CHARING CROSS BOYS

Book Two

Sweet

Caroline

M. KATHERINE CLARK

Prologue

It started just like all the other times. Sixteen-year-old Nigel Sweet hated this place. The older generation hated him because of the color of his skin, the younger generation hated him because of who he was attracted to. He would never understand why his father moved them from their home in the British Virgin Islands to the rainy, dreary, bigoted, London, England. His parents had always supported him, but they didn't understand him. How could they? His father intimidated everyone he met with his nearly six-and-a-half-foot frame and booming Islander accent. Nigel was a scrawny teen going through the clichéd teenage rebellion where black on black on black was all the rage. His black jeans, black T-shirt, and black hooded jumper along with the black and white converse, ratty black nail polish, and a black knit beanie on his head. The only splash of color was the tiny rainbow flag pin on his black backpack.

But that must have been enough. He ignored the racial and sexual slurs from the four boys in the park as long as he could, but they didn't seem to appreciate it. He didn't want a fight. He just wanted to go home to his family, do his homework, and have dinner. He wasn't a threat to them. He didn't affect them in any way. They just wanted to pick a fight and he was the lucky one walking by.

He passed them as quickly as he could, but they followed. The smell of cigarettes and booze easy enough to smell. He wasn't going to get away from them easily. Hiking his backpack higher on his back, Nigel tried to hurry.

Two of the four walked around in front of him, the words coming out of their mouths made Nigel flinch. He had never been called those names and it boiled his blood. When the two stepped in his path, he tried sidestepping them, but they cut him off again. He paused and did not look up at them as he said softly, "please let me through."

"What? Sorry, can't understand you." They leered and tried to mimic his accent.

"I want to get home," he tried again.

"Oh yeah? You wanna know what I want? I want you, you little faggot, to leave and never come back."

"I am certainly trying to. So, if you'll step out of the way."

"You trying to be funny?" One of them gripped his backpack and ripped it off his shoulders.

"Stop!" He shouted as they tore off the rainbow pin.

"Faggot!" One of them shouted and threw it at his face. He blocked the pin with both hands flinching when it embedded itself into his palm.

"Got any other gay things in here?" They unzipped his bag as one of the bigger boys tried to hold him back.

Turning the bag upside down, all Nigel's papers and books fell out including his favorite paperback of Tuck Everlasting, the one his grandmother had given him before she died.

"No please!"

"What's this?" One of the bullies grabbed the book and flipped through it. "Nene? Is that your lover?"

"No! Please!"

The bully flipped the book open to the middle and ripped it down the spine in two tossing the pieces into the mud. Nigel broke away from the one holding him and rushed to the book halves. Tears ran down his cheeks as he saw the slowly fading words on the front page as water bled the ink with his grandmother's final words to him.

Be true to yourself. Always.

Oceans of love, Nene

His whole body shook with anger as the bullies ripped up his tests, projects, essays, and threw his schoolbooks into the mud. Letting out a ferocious yell, Nigel raced to the main bully, the instigator, and tackled him into the mud. He straddled him and threw punch after punch, pummeling the boy's face into the mud. His hands hurt. His heart was broken, but his pain morphed into anger.

The other three grabbed him off the first bully and threw him into another mud pile near his book pieces. He curled into a fetal position holding the book to him as they kicked, spat, and jeered at him. The pain was intense. The hatred suffocated him. He felt hot liquid on his face and realized bully number one was pissing on him as the others kept kicking him and laughing at him.

"What do you think you're doing?" Another voice came from somewhere. "Leave him alone!"

"Gabe! Oh my God!" A female's voice screeched. "They've beaten him to a pulp."

"Call my dad, then get an ambulance," the male voice said. "I'm going after them."

"There now," the female's voice was soft and gentle, and he felt a soft fabric of a jumper wipe his face. "Easy, love. We're going to help you. What's your name?"

But he couldn't answer. He couldn't get a good breath. He heard her voice again, but he didn't think she was talking to him. Finally, the other man's voice came.

"Nance, how is he?"

"He's in and out. Those bastards peed on him, Gabe!" She sounded like she was crying.

"I got one of them. I know who they are. They're in fifth year."

"Why would they do this? It's awful.

"It is. Did you get ahold of my dad? And an ambulance?"

"I did. Your dad is on his way to the hospital and the ambulance is a few minutes out. I'll stay for the police. You go with him to the hospital."

"You sure?"

"Yes," she answered, and he heard the soft sound of a kiss.

"Please," Nigel moaned. "Please."

"Hey, hey, mate," the man's voice was soft. "I'm Gabe. Gabe Collins. What's your name?"

He opened his eyes as much as he could and was greeted by a man, a boy really, in his late teens, dark hair cut short, lazy but intense light green eyes, a kind, open face, and a soft smile.

"Nigel…" he said softly. "My name is Nigel Sweet."

"Nigel, it's all right. I've got you mate." Gabe pressed a hand to Nigel's shoulder. "Try to stay awake, all right?"

But he couldn't and when he opened his eyes again, he was in the hospital with his parents huddled around him and his new friend standing in the doorway. When they locked eyes, Gabe smiled at him, and Nigel felt his heart flutter.

Nigel could finally take a deep breath. The trial was over and he wouldn't need to be there for the sentencing. He took a shuddering breath as he turned his face up to the sky letting the sunshine fall warm on him. His eyes closed, he felt someone walk up to him and smiled when he caught the sweet piney scent of the boy he was falling for.

"In that light you might almost pass as cute, Sweets," Gabe teased, and Nigel loved his nickname for him. No one else could call him that. Only Gabe. His Gabe. Well… not *his* in the way he wanted.

"And in this warm season, you might not pass as gangly."

"Hey, I'll have you know I'm the perfect weight for a wing."

Nigel chuckled. Gabe and his Rugby. "If I didn't know any better I'd say you were going to marry a ball. You love Rugby more than most people love their spouses."

Gabe barked a laugh and Nigel opened his eyes in time to see his wide smile and the sparkle in his eyes. He loved that sparkle. He loved that smile. Gabe's wide carefree look darkened just a bit as he looked at him. Nigel knew what he saw. The scar over his eyebrow was still flaming red from where the bullies had hit him. Reaching forward, Nigel tried not to flinch or lean into his touch when his finger gently caressed the scar.

"You'll look hot with that. You know, most people love scars. I bet you'll get all the guys." Nigel tried to smile. Gabe had known he was gay from the first moment they met, hard to miss the pride flag pin imbedded in his palm. But he had never said anything about it.

Gabe's mother walked over to him and handed Gabe a gift bag as the family surrounded him. Gabe's parents, older brother and younger sister, and Nigel's parents and five-year-old twin sister and brother. Gabe turned back to him.

"So, ehum," he began. "I got you something." He thrust the gift bag in Nigel's direction with a blush staining his cheeks. "It's nothing major. I just saw it in the bookstore one day and thought you might... I don't know, it's stupid. Your parents had a picture of the dedication, and I was able to duplicate it. If you hate it, you can take it back or give it away."

Intrigued, Nigel pulled out the decorative tissue and stared into the bag seeing the familiar cover. He froze staring. His body wouldn't react apart from the tears suddenly swimming in his eyes. Slowly, reverently, he pulled out the paperback of *Tuck Everlasting*. The same cover as the one the bullies tore up. The gift bag hanging from his pinky finger, he opened the cover and his tears fell as a soft sob escaped him.

Be true to yourself. Always.
Oceans of Love, Nene

P.S. I can't tell you how awesome you are and how much I care
about you.
You're the best friend I've ever had. You're like my brother,
only cooler.
Friends forever,
Gabe

Nigel looked up at the man he loved and threw himself at him. Hugging him tightly, he knew it was all he would ever get. Gabe was straight, clearly, as his girlfriend giggled beside him, but in that moment, Nigel could dream.

Summer flew by and even with the vacation back home to the Virgin Islands with the Collins's, Nigel never hated August more than when it came around and Gabe stood in front of him in the airport heading home to pack for college.

"Look, I'm only a phone call away," he said. "France is dope. You should come."

"Yeah, maybe," Nigel replied.

"Your dad said you'd be going back to London in a bit. It's only a couple hours by Chunnel. Promise you'll come to visit."

"I'll... do my best."

Gabe nodded and gouged the linoleum with the toe of his boot. "So... uh," he looked up at him through his lashes and Nigel's heart hammered. "I'll see you around?"

Nigel nodded quickly. "Definitely."

"Ready, Gabe?" his dad called heading toward the gate.

"Yeah," he answered then looked back at Nigel. "Write? Call me?"

"All the above," Nigel promised.

"Cool," he tried to smile and then wrapped his arms around Nigel. Nigel sunk into the heat and scent of his best friend's body. "Always remember, Sweets, I'm here for you."

"Ditto," Nigel replied.

Gabe pulled back and Nigel mourned the connection. With a fond smile, a chuck under the chin, Gabe walked away, leaving Nigel in BVI.

Gabe,

I miss you. I miss you so much. I wish you were here with me. I read under the palm tree again. Or at least tried to. All I kept seeing was you lying in the sun beside me, the palm shade playing with your cheek, the sun drying the droplets of sea water off your skin. The way your hair glistened in the light, so amazing, soft, and beautiful. I really miss you. Sometimes I feel like I can't breathe. Like those bullies are around me again. I know school is breaking for the holidays soon. But I haven't heard from you in a couple of months. I left London. We went back to BVI. I'm staying here for uni. They have a good program. I'm going to be a police officer. I figured it's the least I could do to give back after what happened to me.

You missed my eighteenth birthday. I missed you. I wanted to tell you something. It's taken two years for me to gather the courage to write this letter to you. But Gabe, I love you. I've loved you since the first moment I saw you. I know you're not gay, but I had to tell you. I can't hold this in any longer. I needed to let it out. I needed you to know. I only want what's best for you. So please, don't feel obligated or whatever. Just tell me our relationship can survive this. I don't ask anything from you. *I don't ask you to give me a chance, because you can't help who you're attracted to and I know you don't like guys. But just put my mind and heart at ease and tell me you still care about me? I would never do anything to make you uncomfortable. I just had to tell you.*

Please write back. I've enclosed my new address.

You are the best friend I've ever had. I guess it's only normal to have you be my first love.

Oceans of love,

Your Sweets

Months, then years went by, and Nigel never heard from Gabe again. He knew he had truly lost the only man he'd ever love and his best friend. And it hurt.

London, why did I even come back? Nigel wondered as he walked through the rain to New Scotland Yard.

You know why, stupid, his subconscious said. *You hope to see* him *again.*

Pushing those thoughts out of his mind, he pulled the door open and shook out of his raincoat in the atrium so no one could slip on the linoleum. Checking in, he headed up the stairs to the training room. After five years as a police officer in BVI, he decided he wanted to move on to a more daring career. He spoke to his commissioner, and he'd been put forth as a candidate for the Police Special Operations team and was offered the position as one of fifteen inductees.

"You must be Nigel Sweet," a thick Scottish accent said from behind him as he hung up his raincoat. Turning, he looked up to see who spoke to him. The man was tall with thick muscles but a kind and gentle face, the stripes on the shoulder of his uniform showed he was a higher rank.

"Yes, sir," he answered.

"Rhys Campbell," he introduced himself. "Second Commander. Call me Leo."

"Leo," he shook his hand. "Are you my commander, sir?"

Leo chuckled. "No, not yet, anyway," he winked. "I run the third battalion."

"Oh, I see."

"What brings you from BVI?" he asked as they made their way to seats near the front. "No offense, but I wouldn't give up sunny beach weather for this shite." He hooked his thumb over his shoulder indicating the window and the grey ram clouds beyond.

Nigel laughed and teased. "Yes, it's lovely, isn't it?" Leo let out a laugh. "No, sir, I spent some time in London when I was a boy and there's no chance of advancement in the small parish where I worked. And I was looking for something a little more… exciting."

"Well, we do exciting here but occasionally it's pretty boring. Glad to have you on the team."

"Glad to be here, sir."

"Campbell," another man called him. Leo looked back and nodded.

"Excuse me, boss man waits for no man." With a wink, he walked away, and Nigel decidedly did not look at his ass as he left the area. Nope. He looked away when he caught himself. *Dammit.*

More recruits walked in and soon the room was a cacophony of voices as the men and women milled about. Nigel kept to himself for a time unless someone came up to introduce themselves to him, then he was pleasant enough. He wanted to make friends. But he wasn't sure how. He'd never been particularly good at it. He was friends with people who decided they wanted to be friends with him. Like Gabe used to. Thinking of him invariably brought the heartache. He had never responded to his letter. He had never spoken to him again. With a sigh, he forced his thoughts away from the man but as if the universe was toying with him, he heard his laugh. Looking up, his brows furrowed.

There it was again.

His head swiveled around and there, by the tea trolly, like his mind conjured him, stood Gabriel Collins. The man Nigel loved. All color drained out of his face, his lips tingled, and his body went limp. Gabe was in the room. He was laughing at something someone said. His Gabe. Older, but those years looked damn good on him. His hair was still that dark silky color, his aquamarine eyes were still vibrant even if the skin around them crinkled more than before. His lips, those perfect pink lips were turned up into his signature dazzling grin. Before he knew what he was doing, Nigel stood and made his way over. His eyes glued to the man as if afraid if he looked away he would be gone. He stood behind him, certain he looked like a stalker and hesitantly cleared his throat.

"Gabe?" he questioned.

The man who saved his life. The man he dreamt about for years. The one who had his teenage heart all aflutter, turned that blindingly beautiful smile to him. Confusion crossed his eyes, then surprise, and finally recognition.

"Sweets?" he questioned, and Nigel couldn't help the grin that spread across his face. He was back ten years ago lying on the sand, the sun beating down on him as he gazed at his best friend lying beside him, the waters of the Caribbean Sea washing over their feet keeping them cool. "Oh my God, Sweets!"

Setting down his coffee, Gabe grabbed him into his massive chest. Nigel went willingly and wrapped his arms around his back. He was home. Taking a deep inhale of Gabe's scent, so many memories from his teenage years flooded back to him.

Gabe pulled back too quickly for Nigel's taste but the smile that greeted him was perfect. "Is it really you?"

"Yeah," Nigel shrugged.

"What are you doing here?"

"I'm a new recruit. Spent some time back home in the Virgin Islands as a police officer then transfer back to London."

"I looked for you when I came home from Uni, mate. I couldn't find you," Gabe said.

"Didn't you get my letter?"

"Letter?"

"Oh shite, really? I explained everything." *And confessed my love for you.*

"I didn't get anything," he answered.

"You must think I'm a bastard just leaving like that with no goodbye?" *Just like I thought you were when you didn't respond to my confession.*

"No! Of course not! Mate, I'm sorry, there was a house fire while my parents were in Nice, and I guess maybe it got destroyed?"

"Oh, I'm sorry about the house."

"Yeah, lost a lot of stuff. But tell me what's happened with you? It's been ten years!" Gabe ran his left hand through his hair and Nigel's eyes landed on the shiny piece of metal wrapped around his ring finger. His heart lurched. His brain short circuited. He stared until Gabe lowered his hand.

"You're married." It was more a statement than a question. The evidence was hard to ignore.

"Yeah, I got a little boy, Hunter and another on the way," he bragged.

After a long moment, knowing he needed to say something, Nigel cleared his throat and forced, "congratulations!" The walls were closing in. He could hear the bullies taunting him. Feel the soft arms wrap around him. "I'm sure you and Nancy are very happy."

"Nancy? God no, mate that ended," he blew a raspberry "eons ago. No, Amelie and I met in France."

"Oh."

To lose him to Nancy, he was prepared for. She was sweet, kind, and gentle. She would have been a perfect wife. But to lose him to someone completely unknown was not something Nigel had been prepared for. Swallowing around the lump in his throat, he smiled, was properly apologetic for assuming, and properly happy for his happiness. When Gabe was called away by another member of the team and told Nigel they'd grab a beer at the pub that evening, Nigel took his chance and ran to the nearest toilet. Locking the door, he sat on the commode, wrapped his arm around his torso, and wept.

He would never have him. He knew that. Gabe Collins was straight. Never once looked at Sweet in any way that made him question his cast iron sexuality. But still. To have found him again after all this time, only to have the door firmly shut in his face, that hurt.

He hoped Gabe was happy. That was all he ever wanted for him.

Chapter

One

Six Years Later

Gabe stared at his wife wrapped in the silk negligee he had bought for her for their last wedding anniversary. Her hair messed and a freshly forming hickey appearing on her neck, as the man moved around their bedroom gathering his clothes.

"How? How could you cheat on me?" Gabe breathed.

The man hurried to the door and left without a second glance. Amelie said nothing, only sat at her dressing table, reapplying her lipstick.

"Don't pretend this isn't your fault, Gabriel," she said. Her English was perfect when she wanted it to be but her French accent still colored the words.

"My fault?" He demanded.

"*Oui,* you're always gone with that team of yours doing god knows what."

"Saving England? The empire? The whole damn world!"

"Don't raise your voice to me," she said.

"You cheated on me with my sons in the next room!" He shouted. "Don't talk to me about raising my damn voice."

"And they are awake now thanks to you. They never woke while they were here."

"*They?* How many men were there?" He yelled.

She stood and walked over to him. "I told you not to yell at me."

"And you made vows before god to be faithful to me! You're my wife!"

Gabe felt her slap rather than saw it. His cheek stung. He honestly couldn't believe it. Breathing a laugh, he looked back at her. She had sauntered to the window and gazed out of the curtain. Gabe stared at her for a long moment taking in how he felt. His parents had been married over fifty years, his brother and sister-in-law had fifteen years under their belt, his baby sister was going on five years with her boyfriend. And he was in the middle with Amelie. They were eleven years in with an eleven and a six-year-old.

Commitment. Honor. Love. Those were the three foundations of a marriage, weren't they? That's what his father had said in his wedding speech. She didn't want the commitment. She didn't honor him. And love? That was a laugh. Their love had fizzled out a long time ago if it ever actually existed. They were in lust, made a mistake, and he married her to give his child a name. Was he a horrible person for thinking his thoughts? He didn't care at that moment.

"Get your bags, I want you out of my house before I get back."

She turned to look at him, the shock evident on her face. "And just where do you expect me to go?"

"I don't give a damn, Ami. Go to your mother's. Go to one of the dozens of men you shared our bed with. Just get out and expect divorce papers in the mail."

"Don't you dare put this on me," she said.

"I'm not the one who had the affairs, Amelie! You are. Do you honestly expect me to take you back? I want you out. Out of my life. Out of our boys' lives. You were never there anyway."

"Daddy?" His eldest son's voice came from behind him. He turned to see both his boys standing in the doorway.

"Heya, lads," he breathed.

"We heard shouting," his youngest said.

"Sorry, Colt. *Maman* is going to go stay with *grand-mère* for a short time, all right?" Gabe said.

"Are we going too?" Colton, his youngest, asked.

"No no, you're going to stay with me. Is that all right with you?"

The boys nodded emphatically. And apparently that was enough for Amelie to lose it. She launched herself at Gabe, scratching, kicking, biting even.

"Hunter, get a bag, grab some clothes and your school uniforms and get your brother out of here," Gabe ordered. "Wait for me by the car."

Amelie was insane, that was the only description. Shouting obscenities at him in French and English as she used her nails to scratch his face. The cut above his eye was particularly painful. Fending her off, he met his sons outside.

"What's wrong with *maman*, daddy?" Colton whimpered.

"I don't know, Colt." He put the car in gear and pulled slowly out of the driveway.

"I didn't grab my football uniform for tomorrow's practice, daddy. I'm sorry," his eldest said.

"Hey buddy, tomorrow's a long way off. I'll come back and get your stuff," Gabe replied.

"Where are we going?" Colton asked.

Gabe stopped at the end of their neighborhood road and contemplated. Then, an idea came to him, "we're going to your godfather's."

Nigel had just turned off the lamp beside his reading chair. He had come home after the mission, debrief, and celebratory pub dinner and drinks with his team and collapsed into his favorite chair. Putting on some Dark Academia music on YouTube to calm his mind after being bait in the *Honeypot* con they pulled off, he read his favorite author's new fantasy gay romance book for over an hour.

The latest mission with his new team, The Charing Cross Boys, MI6's latest off-the-books assets was nerve wracking but easier than he expected. A group of them, five field operatives, one boss, and their team's admin created a tight group especially when everyone on the team was skilled, smart, and gay like him. Well, he chuckled to himself, not *everyone* on the team was gay. Gabe Collins, his police partner and best friend was straight, married, and a dad of two of the sweetest little boys to ever exist. But he was an Ally and treated like one of the boys even if he had never kissed a bloke before. Sweet would actively raise his hand as volunteer if ever Gabe wanted to change that particular fact.

Sighing, he took his wine glass to the counter and glanced at the clock. It was still technically early for him at 2200, but he was beat. He headed to the bathroom to wash his face and prepare his nightly routine when his doorbell sounded. His brows furrowed as he checked his phone still on silent from when he was reading. He had three missed texts from Gabe.

Gabe: You home?

Gabe: Sorry, I know this is random, but could the boys and I crash at your place tonight?

Gabe: I'll explain everything.

Hurrying to the front door, he opened it to see Gabe and his boys standing outside.

"Hey, sorry, my phone was off. Come on in. Hey boys!"

"Hi, Uncle Nige," the eldest said but his voice was quiet, almost sad.

"Did something happen? To the house? To Amelie?" He glanced up at Gabe and saw the claw marks on his face and a red angry mark on his cheek.

"*Maman* and Daddy are getting a divorce," Colton said.

Sweet's eyes widened. "What?"

"Come on boys, let's get inside," Gabe said. Colton rushed to Nigel and threw his arms around his waist, burying his face in Sweet's stomach. Nigel hugged him back and crouched down to be eye level with the little boy.

"I have some of those chocolate biscuits you like in the larder. Help yourself."

Colton sniffled but nodded and walked over to the kitchen as Hunter sat on the sofa and turned on the television.

"Bed in an hour, boys," Gabe called. Then, turning to Nigel he gave a tired smile. "Thanks for this."

"Of course, you're all always welcome here."

Nigel reached up to touch around Gabe's cut on his eyebrow. "Let's get that looked at. Come on."

A minute later, Gabe sat on the toilet seat while Nigel stood over him dabbing a cotton ball on the cut.

"I wasn't sure if you'd be… entertaining. Hence the texts," Gabe said.

Nigel chuckled. "Not on a school night," he winked. "I usually am my best company when I have a 0800 meeting in the morning."

"Good to know," Gabe replied then hissed as the alcohol stung.

"Sorry," he paused. "You going to tell me what happened?" Nigel asked continuing to clean the cut.

Gabe let out a sigh that broke Nigel's heart. "I found her cheating on me."

Nigel paused, blinked at him, then questioned, "are you serious?" *How could that bitch do that?* He wanted to shout.

"Yep, the boys were in their room asleep. I got home after our dinner and found her in our bed with another man. The bloke flipped when he saw me."

"Obviously," Nigel agreed. Not only did Gabe look like an MMA fighter, but he was also still wearing his tactical gear from earlier.

"Then she accused me of leaving her alone to fend for herself or something like that. Then, when I raised my voice, which I know I shouldn't have-"

"Uh huh, don't do that. Don't blame yourself. You were angry."

"Yeah," he breathed. "But she slapped me. That's when I realized."

Nigel was pissed but he kept his feelings to himself as he placed the butterfly bandage over the cut. "Realized what?"

"That I didn't care." Gabe let out a pitiful moan and Nigel stepped back, giving him room. "I've been lying to myself and her for so long. I don't think I've ever... I know I loved her or at least I should have. She is the mother of my boys. But there's always been this... disconnect. Like with you, you always know what I'm thinking or how I'm feeling. You get me. She just... doesn't. I don't think she ever did."

Nigel refused to allow his words to affect him. He meant nothing by them. Pulling himself out of his thoughts, he focused on what Gabe was saying.

"...and then it was like this epiphany. We built our marriage on necessity, not love. But then I thought about my parents, and Frank and Sarah, and I realized, I'm a failure."

At the mention of his brother and sister, Gabe looked down. Nigel crouched low and cupped his face forcing him to look at him. "Don't do that to yourself. They have their relationships, you have yours. You cannot judge yours based on theirs. You don't know what their marriage is truly like. You see what they want you to see. Same with how you and Amelie presented your marriage to them. You are not a failure, Gabe," Nigel promised.

"No, I am. Something must be wrong with me if I can't make my marriage work. I'm a failure as a man, a husband, and a father."

"Now, wait just one damn minute." Nigel stood in front of him again making him look up. "I will not allow that sort of talk. You are not at fault here."

"But I must be. She was looking for something I couldn't provide, so she looked elsewhere."

"No, she looked elsewhere because *she* wanted to look elsewhere," Nigel stated.

Gabe sighed harshly. "Tell me something, Nigel," he began. One of the few times Gabe called him by his first name versus *Sweets*. "I know you wouldn't lie to me."

"Never."

"Am I... unlovable? Emotionally unavailable? Do I smother people? Tell me, am I a horrible person?" Gabe's eyes pleaded with him, and the pain hidden behind them caused tears to pool in Nigel's eyes. He licked his lips and crouched again to be on the same level with him. He cupped Gabe's jaw and locked eyes with the man he had loved since he was sixteen.

"Gabriel Collins," he began. "You are the best man I have ever known. Your kindness, strength, beauty, personality, and love are second to none. You have so much to give and if she can't see that, she doesn't deserve you. You are an amazing man, friend, brother-in-arms, and father to those boys. There are so many people who love you. Me, included." His heart sped with his declaration. Gabe cracked a small smile.

"Thank you. I love you too," he said, and Nigel tried to keep his face neutral. Gabe had told him he loved him like a friend or a brother so many times, but it still stung even after all those years.

"Now," he lowered his hand and stood. "I've got some wine in the fridge, but it'll be too sweet for you. I have some gin and whiskey in the liquor cabinet. What can I get you?"

"A small whiskey maybe to help me sleep, but I've got to get the boys to school in the morning and we've got that meeting at 0800. Then, I have to swing by the house to get Hunter's uniform for his practice tomorrow."

"Do you want to go back there alone?"

"Not particularly." He motioned to his face and Nigel's hand clenched.

"She did that?"

"Yeah, but she was different. Like, it wasn't her, you know? She just flew at me."

"Talk to Kiter or Leo tomorrow and see what they think?" Nigel offered. "Leo" codename and alternate name for Rhys Campbell, was their boss on the force. Kiter, their current boss of The Charing Cross Boys, was Rhys' boyfriend.

"I don't want to bring them into it," Gabe said. "They have enough to worry about. And we're meeting the new recruit tomorrow. It's not the best time to talk about what the job has done to my family life. I'll talk to my dad and see what he says."

"Good idea," Nigel said. "Come on, I'm sure the boys are probably worried. The guest room has clean sheets."

"I'll sleep on the couch," Gabe offered.

"Not sure you remember how uncomfortable my couch is." Nigel offered his hand and helped Gabe stand.

"Hunter's probably already asleep on it. I can share the guest room with Colton."

"All right, if that works for you."

"It does for now. I'll have to figure out what to do next," Gabe said thrusting his fingers through his hair. "I told her to get out, but I seriously doubt she will."

"You know you can stay here, no matter what," Nigel said. "For however long you need."

Gabe's lips quirked into a half smile. He looked so tired. "Thanks, Sweets. I owe you one."

"Nothing is owed. That's what friends do."

With a gentle touch on Nigel's upper arm, Gabe left the bathroom and Nigel cleaned up the slightly bloody cotton balls, waste from the plaster, and the ointment he had put on the cut. He needed to calm his thoughts. Gabe had always looked out for him ever since he was a boy. He had been his partner on the police force and defended him against their own colleague Bethel who had picked a fight with Nigel and beaten him up a couple months ago.

Sweet never had a chance to return all those favors to Gabe, until then. But he couldn't very easily hurt Amelie, that wasn't how he worked, no matter how much he wanted to. But to see the pain in Gabe's eyes, Nigel knew he would do anything in his power to save his best friend and the love of his life.

Now Available!

www.ingramcontent.com/pod-product-compliance
Lightning Source LLC
Chambersburg PA
CBHW052034020726
47501CB00004B/1396